ONE WISH

Cassie Edwards Whitlow

Dedication

To Eric, my husband, my biggest supporter, my number one fan. Also to my baby loves Nathan and Krista. You guys bring me joy.

Acknowledgments

To my Lord and Savior Jesus Christ who makes the impossible possible.

My mom and friend. You've always lived the life you you've preached about. Thank you for being the constant in my life. Thank you for your presence and your encouragement. You've always told me that if anyone else can do it, so can I. The same God who anointed them, has anointed me also. I love you.

My sister Keidra, who always has my back, even when I'm wrong. And my brother Darius, thanks for beating up all the kids that used to pick on me on the bus.

Authors and Literary Supporters: **Stacy Hawkins Adams** and the *Focused Writers Community.* **Stacy**, I credit your novel, "Watercolored Pearls" for sparking my love for reading that would eventually lead to my love for writing. **Rhonda McKnight** for teaching me everything I know about writing and thanks for not blocking me from your Facebook inbox. **Victoria Christopher Murray** for your fabulous writing workshop. You taught me so much in such a short amount of time. **Jacqueline Owensby**, my coach, mentor, and friend. You encouraged me to start journaling. Once I finally listened, I discovered how much a really enjoyed writing. Thank you for your encouragement over the past few years. **Felicia Murrell**, You are the best editor God has ever created. You make me shine. Ladies you've been with me throughout this journey and I appreciate each of you for different reasons. You've taught me a lot.

Other authors who've inspired me: Vanessa Miller, Jacquelin Thomas, EN Joy, Brenda Barrett, Reshonda Tate Billingsley, Pat Simmons, Michelle Stimpson, Piper Huguley, Tia McCollors, Tiffany L. Warren, Sherri Lewis, Shawneda Marks, Michelle Lindo Rice, H H Fowler, Kimberla Lawson Roby, LaShaunda Hoffman, Unoma Nwankor, and Alesha Brown.

To my aunts, uncles, cousins, nieces, and nephews. My friends, social media crew, and fans. Without you, my stories would go unread. Your support keeps me going. I appreciate each of you.

ONE WISH

Cassie Edwards Whitlow

Prologue

(Christmas Eve 2009)

Iman bolted straight up in bed. She squeezed her eyes shut, opened them, and repeated until her vision became clear. Finally able to take in her surroundings, she remembered she was at her grandparents' home. Struggling to regulate her heartbeat, Iman turned her attention to the sound of the ringing phone. She glanced at the space next to her, checking to see if the intrusion had awakened her husband. To her surprise, he wasn't there.

The clock read 3 a.m. She yanked the covers off the bed and tossed the pillows onto the floor. When she still didn't see her phone, she flipped the light switch and followed the sound to the dresser on the other side of the room. She went to reach for it and knocked it behind the dresser. With a loud, frustrated grunt, Iman pulled the dresser from against the wall, kneeled onto the floor, reached behind it, and pulled the phone out.

By the time she'd gotten to it, the ringing had stopped. She frowned and wondered why her cousin Tiana, who should have been asleep in the next room, was calling her. She figured it must have been a mistake, so she didn't call back.

Still feeling uneasy about Cedric not being in bed, she looked out the window to see if their car was gone. It was still parked in the driveway.

Finally able to catch her breath, she flopped down onto the bed. He was probably in the bathroom or still downstairs playing cards with her uncles. It was tradition that everyone gathered at Iman's grandmother's house in Augusta to celebrate Christmas together.

Iman had three great aunts and two great uncles who still lived in the area, but most of the family opted to stay at her grandmother's. Not only was there more space, Vivian Braswell went above and beyond to assure everyone felt at home. Tiana's mother lived only three blocks away. Why she always felt the need to stay at Vivian's was a mystery.

Iman and Cedric had been there three days and were leaving for Montego Bay the next day to celebrate their one-year anniversary. Iman's grandmother didn't understand why anyone would get married on Christmas Day. She'd often said Christmas was to be celebrated with the whole family and not a day to celebrate a wedding anniversary. They'd compromised and told her they'd spend the days leading up to Christmas with the family.

One Wish

Iman had chosen to marry on Christmas, in hopes of creating pleasant memories, instead of dreading it as she'd done for years. She was born three days before Christmas. Her mother died on Christmas Day of the same year. Three days after her third birthday, her father was found dead in an alley. It would be three years ago tomorrow that her grandfather had died of a heart attack. Needless to say, the holidays didn't mean to her what it meant to most. Although she had a lot of bad memories about Christmas, Iman was determined to do whatever she could to create better memories.

Iman's family believed in making a big ordeal during the holidays. She'd be lying if she said she didn't enjoy staying up late cooking and reminiscing with her grandma, great aunts, and cousins, while the men watched football and argued over whose team was better.

The older women always tackled the meat and side dishes, while the younger women made desserts. Iman lived for pecan and sweet potato pies. The best part was the singing. Every woman on Iman's mother's side of the family could sing. The harmony that sounded through their kitchen when they sang *I'll Be Home for Christmas* and *Silent Night* could put the Braxton Sisters to shame.

With the exception of Tiana, whose birth name was Tina, Iman got along well with her entire family. As far back as Iman could remember, Tiana hated her birth name. She always said, as soon as she became an adult, she would change it. Tiana was three years older than Iman, and they'd gotten along fine until around the time Iman was a freshman and Tiana a senior year in high school.

Iman was raised by her maternal grandparents. Tiana's mother, Helen, and Iman's grandmother, Vivian, were sisters. Tiana was the surprise baby, born when her mother was in her late forties. She was the youngest of eight children. Both being raised by older parents, they found comfort in having one another to deal with their old fashioned upbringing without going insane.

One day, for some unknown reason, Tiana started ignoring her and making fun of her in front of her classmates. Still, Iman called and attempted to find out what she'd done to make Tiana treat her that way. After a few weeks, she realized their close relationship was over.

Cedric didn't seem to need much sleep. Iman, however, believed in getting as close to eight hours as possible. To avoid any more unwanted interruptions, Iman switched the sound on her phone to vibrate, placed it on the nightstand, turned the lights off, and crawled back into bed.

No sooner than she'd dozed back off, the sound of her phone vibrating lulled her from her sleep. Now, she was concerned. Tiana was calling her again. She clicked the answer button on her iPhone. If Tiana was calling her this late, something must be wrong.

One Wish

Tiana never called. She wondered why her number was even in her contacts. It certainly shouldn't have been in her call log. She braced herself for the worse before she answered.

"Hello, Ti—"

Iman looked at her phone with disgust and rolled her eyes. The sound of heavy breathing clued her to what Tiana was up to. One finger hovered over the end button until she heard Tiana say, "Oooh, Cedric. You always know just how I like it."

A muffled male's voice could be heard groaning in the background. Iman shook her head. *No. It couldn't be.*

Cedric was a common name. Surely, this wasn't her Cedric. They'd had their share of problems over the past few months, but they'd been together since high school. And he wouldn't dare mess around with her cousin, especially with her family around. But still, something inside her wouldn't allow her to end the call. She sat down on the side of the bed and listened.

"Sneaking around like this where someone could catch us at any minute turns me on so much. And you know how I love the new car smell."

New Car? Iman stood and ran to the window. "Not the Range Rover he just bought me." She strained her eyes, but the windows were tinted too dark to see anything.

Inhaling deeply, Iman squeezed her eyes shut. Was Tiana really with her husband? At her family's home? The home she'd grown up in? She wouldn't put it past Tiana, but Cedric was better than that.

Iman was anything but naïve. She'd suspected Cedric a few times but could never prove it. It'd been five months since he'd touched her romantically. A month after her miscarriage, he'd stopped sleeping with her. She assumed it was because the doctors said her chance of carrying a child full-term was low. She knew Cedric wanted children almost as much as she did.

Had he been with Tiana all this time? Tired of hearing him grunt and Tiana moan, she disconnected the call and dialed Cedric. The call went to voicemail without ringing.

Iman's face started to burn. Her heart beat rapidly. She paced back and forth from the bed to the window. Refusing to allow even one tear to escape, Iman was determined to get answers.

Iman refused to waste any time feeling sorry for herself. She looked outside once more. This time, she noticed fumes coming from the tail pipe. "These fools are having sex in my car."

Grabbing her robe and slippers, Iman scurried out of the room. She grabbed one of her grandfather's golf clubs from the storage closet before walking outside. She'd worked hard to recreate herself as sophisticated and classy, but there was a little bit of hood aching to be unleashed.

With quick measured steps, Iman sneaked up on the car, not bothering to peek inside. There was no need to. She'd heard Tiana loud and clear in her description.

Without giving her conscience time to talk her out of it, she started swinging the golf club. First, she busted out the windshield. Cedric jumped up, knocking Tiana onto the floor. He quickly tried to cover himself with his shirt. He scrambled clumsily, pulling both legs of his jeans up at the same time.

Satisfied with his startled reaction, she moved to the back window, where only seconds ago they were going at it like wild animals. Iman swung the golf club, moving around the car with swiftness until she'd busted every piece of glass in sight.

Dressed in only a tank top and some booty shorts she'd just pulled up, Tiana's eyes bucked. She swiftly moved to the opposite side of Iman and her golf club, opened the door, and jumped out. "Have you lost your mind?"

Iman shook her head. "No." She held the club up in one hand and started towards Tiana. "But I'm about to lose a cousin."

The scowl on Iman's face was enough to cause Tiana to step back. She moved back just in time to bump into Cedric, who'd just stepped out of the car. He quickly pushed her off of him and stepped closer to Iman.

"Iman, calm down. I can—"

"Don't you dare fix your lips to say you can explain," she yelled. Iman pointed the club in his direction, causing him to freeze.

She glanced at Tiana, who was now leaned up against the house. Iman wondered what type of flesh the girl was created with. Tiana wasn't even shivering in the below 30-degree weather and if she didn't know any better, Iman could've sworn she saw a smirk on her face.

She wondered if Tiana's phone call was an accident. *Had she wanted me to catch them?*

"Baby, I swear. It was nothing." Cedric reached for Iman's arm. "It didn't mean anything. She forced—"

Iman swung the golf club wildly as hard as she could, not caring whose head it connected with. If Cedric hadn't ducked, she probably would have cracked his skull. She hadn't planned to cause physical harm to anyone when she first grabbed the club, but the more Cedric talked, the more she felt her control slipping away.

"What is wrong with you? You're acting like a crazy—"

"You haven't seen crazy." She chased him around the car as he ducked and dodged.

"Mimi, stop!" Iman's head turned at the sound of her grandmother's voice. Her uncle James and cousin Anthony approached her.

"This fool ain't worth you out here actin like this," her uncle said.

"Yeah," Anthony said. "That's my job." With a face full of venom, he stared at Cedric.

"Put the club down and let's go inside," Vivian said.

At some point during the commotion, Tiana either left or went inside because she was nowhere in sight.

Iman fixed a shaken Cedric with a disgusted look. Her entire family was standing around looking on. Without acknowledging their presence, she headed towards the front door and threw down the club. "I hate Christmas."

"Now Unto Him that is able to do exceeding abundantly above all that we ask or think, according to the power that worketh in us."

Ephesians 3:20 (KJV)

Chapter One

(Seven Years Later)

"Never again."

Iman squeezed her eyes shut to try and stop the tears from escaping. She snatched her hand from her husband of three years, turned her back to him, and wiped her eyes.

Inhaling deeply, Iman turned her attention to the Christmas tree and all the decorations they'd put up a week before. "I knew better than to get my hopes up."

She stormed off towards the family room and stopped in front of the Christmas tree. She snatched the ornaments off one by one, throwing them onto the floor, not caring where they landed or if they broke. She wanted to get rid of every trace of Christmas. She'd succeeded in avoiding the Christmas hoopla six years straight, escaping to one tropical island after another. But not this year. She must have been a fool to think this year would be different.

"We'll get through this," Micah said. "We always do."

She faced him with a scowl. “We? You didn’t attempt to stop them. Do you even care that they’re gone?”

“Of course I care. You know I do. I love them just as much as you.”

“You have a funny way of showing it. You didn’t say a word to the social worker. You could’ve talked them out of taking them. I swear I’m going to die alone.”

He looked at her like she’d lost her mind. “What do you mean you’re going to die alone? I’m not going anywhere and as for having children, there are other options.”

“I would love to hear them.” She pulled the lights from the tree, causing it to spin in a circle. “Because so far, our options have done nothing except left me heartbroken.”

With one sweep, she cleared the garland and fake snow off the mantle. “I’ve been waiting to adopt for years and your idea of being foster parents… well, look around,” she spread her hands out, “you see where that’s gotten us. You’re against surrogacy. So tell me, Dr. Micah Carrington,” she leaned her back onto the wall and folded her arms, “what do you suggest?”

Micah sighed and sat on the arm of the couch. “You know how I feel about using a surrogate. I don’t want some stranger carrying our child. There have been too many stories that didn’t end well.”

She unfolded her arms and let them fall to her side. “It doesn’t have to be a stranger. We can get someone we know to do it, like a family member."

"What family?" Micah frowned. "My sister, Hannah isn't an option because she's only been in remission from Leukemia for a little over a year and the only cousins I have are guys. And you don't have any siblings. The only female cousins you have... well, I'm sure you don't want to use any of them."

As much as she hated to admit it, Micah was right. She wouldn't think of asking any of her cousins that were childbearing age. Leslie already had four children and the last two were via cesarean and she said she'd never go through that again. Denise was an alcoholic and Tiana no longer existed as far as Iman was concerned.

"We've tried in-vitro twice, against your doctor's advice," he paused, "and mine. I can't watch you go through that again."

"Well, Micah." Iman stood up straight. "Everything isn't about what you can and can't watch. I'm not a fragile little girl. I know what I can handle."

"There are so many children in the foster care system that need us. Why not just get another family?"

"Because I don't want temporary children," she yelled and threw her hands up. "I want my own. Mine." She patted her chest. "And no one can take them from me," she lowered her voice to a whisper. "Why don't you get that?" Dropping her face into both of her hands, she squeezed her eyes tight but couldn't control the tears from flowing.

Iman was all for adopting. She'd updated her information into the database every six months for the past six years. She only stopped once she became a foster mom. But, after experiencing the heartbreak of having them taken away from her, the only way she'd ever take on foster children again was if the parents were both deceased and there was no other family around.

"I do get it." Micah stood and moved closer to his wife. He reached out in attempt to comfort her. When she resisted, he reached over and grabbed a few Kleenex from the end table, handed them to her, and gave her time to collect her thoughts.

After a few moments, Iman wiped her tears and took a few deep breaths. "There are surrogacy agencies out there. They'll do the background checks and we can get a lawyer and—"

"No." Micah closed his eyes and shook his head. "We're not using a surrogate."

They stared at each other without saying a word. Iman struggled to keep her tears at bay. After realizing she could no longer control them, she turned and walked out of the room.

"Iman," he said. "Where are you going?"

Despite hearing her husband's plea to stay and talk with him, she dragged her body upstairs to their bedroom, closed the door, and locked it. She leaned her back against the door and stared at the wall.

Earlier that day, Maya, Iman's best friend, broke the news that their foster children's mother was out of jail and would be getting them back. Iman was grateful to her for taking control and giving her the news personally. She appreciated even more so that it was Maya and not the children's normal social worker. Iman wasn't fond of Alana Smith's condescending attitude.

"Lord, why does everything have to be so hard? Why can't I have a normal life like everyone else? I'm a good person. I don't ask for much. You took my mother before I was a week old. My dad drank himself to death by the time I was three. All I've ever wanted was a house full of beautiful healthy children."

"Baby." Micah knocked on the door. "Don't shut me out. I don't mean to sound unreasonable. I want you to be happy, but I'll be fine if it's just us for the rest of our lives. I don't believe surrogacy is the answer. Let's take some time and pray on it. Okay?"

Iman released a soft sigh and slid down the wall onto the floor. She wasn't in the mood to talk to Micah, God, or anyone else. Her anger was misguided, but what she needed was to be left alone. "I'll be fine, Micah. I just need some time."

"Okay, baby. I'll be downstairs if you need me. I love you." A few moments passed before Micah walked away.

Iman couldn't understand what she did to deserve the cards life had dealt her. It couldn't have been anything she'd done wrong. Was she being punished for her parents' past transgressions? Does that really happen? She'd had her life planned out ever since she was twelve and she'd followed it to the letter. She'd keep her grades up throughout high school, get a full paid academic scholarship and earn a Bachelor's degree in Criminal Justice and a Master's in Counseling Psychology. She'd work at least two years and then marry Cedric, her high school sweetheart, and have her first child before she turned thirty.

She'd gone slightly off course after her grandfather died but, other than that, her plan had gone perfectly. That was, until her first miscarriage. Not only did she learn her chances of having children were slim, but she'd lost her husband in the process. She didn't think she'd be childless and on her second husband at thirty-four.

She thanked God every day for Micah. He was one of the good ones. He'd never been unfaithful, made more than enough money as an oncologist to support them, and he'd do almost anything to make her happy. But didn't they all start off that way?

In hopes that he would run and never return, Iman had revealed to Micah during their first date that she couldn't bear children. She'd only gone out with him because of a bet she'd lost with Maya, who'd forced her to go on a blind date as payment. Iman had thrown everything she could to turn Micah off, but the harder she pushed, the more he fought to win her over. In the end, he'd won.

After Iman's first marriage went sour, she realized she wasn't getting any younger. It didn't matter if she had a man in her life or not. That wasn't and still isn't on her list of priorities. She didn't need one to take care of her financially, nor did she need one to have a child.

Just as she'd made up her mind that she'd take matters into her own hands by attempting to adopt, she'd do the same now. Iman was tired of waiting for adoption agencies. After three miscarriages and two failed in-vitro attempts, some women would give up, but not Iman. There was always another way, and she'd always have a new plan.

As much as she loved her husband, he didn't understand. How could he? He'd had the privilege of growing up with both parents, siblings, and cousins who were still like brothers to him. He didn't fear waking up one day and not having anyone. Three or four children would insure that didn't happen to Iman. She didn't care what Micah said; she would search out reputable agencies and find a surrogate on her own. Once he saw how happy she was, he'd come around. He'd gotten over it when she'd made the in-vitro appointment and he'd just have to jump on board with this plan.

Chapter *Two*

"I stabbed Trish in the arm with my box cutter." Sharell leaned forward, resting her elbow on the table with her chin cupped in her hand.

"Mmmmm. That's nice." Iman stared blankly across the table.

Sharell relaxed back into her chair. "Next time, I'll probably just shoot her."

Iman blinked. "What?"

Sharell shook her head and laughed. "You wilin', Mrs. Carrington. "You ain't heard nothing I said to you since I been sittin' hea."

Iman grimaced. With the tough teens she dealt with, she couldn't risk being distracted.

"It's time for group." Leah, another counselor walked inside. She spoke to Sharell but kept her gaze on Iman. "Mr. Hall is waiting outside the door with the rest of the group."

Iman stood abruptly and exited the room behind Sharell.

"You okay? What's going on?" Leah didn't waste any time following Iman into the break room. Iman liked Leah well enough. They often ate lunch together and chatted during breaks, but that was as far as their relationship went. Leah usually did most of the sharing.

"I'm fine. Why do you ask?" Iman wasn't in the mood to get into a long, drawn out conversation about her childless life. It was nothing she hadn't heard before.

"I'm asking because each time I've seen you today, you've been staring into space and that's not like you." Leah leaned onto the counter next to Iman. "I've been keeping an eye out because I didn't want you distracted while dealing with these knuckleheads." She grabbed the saltshaker from Iman's hand. "And because you're putting salt in your coffee."

Iman looked into her cup and rolled her eyes to the ceiling. She walked over and threw the cup into the trash. Looking around at the pink and blue decor, Iman swallowed the lump that formed in her throat anytime she was reminded of just how empty she felt inside.

"I forgot to get Rita a gift. What did you get her?" Iman hoped Leah caught the message that she didn't want to talk.

Leah looked at her for a moment and then finally responded. "I got her a gift card. I don't like picking out gifts for other people. I figure they know what they want; they can get it themselves."

It was difficult enough that Iman didn't wake up to the three familiar faces she'd grown accustomed to seeing for the past five months. She wasn't sure if she could bear sitting through an hour-long baby shower after work and pretend to be happy for a co-worker who was due to give birth to twins in two months.

"They're all in group right now. If you want, we can run out and get her something together. I need to get out of here and get some air anyway."

Iman had tried all morning to conjure a good enough excuse as to why she couldn't make the shower. She'd just have to suck it up and pray it went by quickly. "Yeah, sure." Iman shrugged. "Let's get out of here."

Iman felt Leah's eyes on her but refused to look in her direction. She'd practiced her stoic face during the ride to Babies R Us. She hoped she could pull it off. If that didn't work, small talk might. "So many choices, I'm not sure where to begin."

She walked up and down the aisles in a daze. *Why did I choose this store?* It seemed every aisle Iman walked down, there were pregnant women who looked like they were almost ready to give birth. She walked ahead of Leah to another aisle and ended up in the 4T sizes. She picked up a tutu and brought it to her chest. It was identical to the one she'd purchased for Kendall, the youngest of the three foster children, the week before they left. She was supposed to wear it for their Christmas pictures.

Feeling weak, Iman sat on a nearby stool and let her head rest against the wall.

"Would you rather I do this for you?" Leah walked up and kneeled in front of her. "Go on out to the car and I'll get a few things."

"No." Iman sniffed and shook her head. "I can do it."

Leah pulled her into a hug when Iman's sniff turned into big sobs.

"My babies," Iman said.

"What about them?"

"They're gone. Social worker came and got them yesterday afternoon."

"I had no idea. Why didn't you say anything?"

Iman shrugged. "I'm trying not to think about it. It's just so hard." She grabbed a handful of Kleenex from her purse and patted her face. "I'm not getting any younger. Everyone around me is either done having children or pregnant with their second or third. By the time I get a call from the adoption agency, I'll be too old to enjoy them. If it's a newborn, I'll be going on sixty when they graduate."

Leah didn't respond.

"Is God punishing me? Does He not want me to have children? I'm not picky. It doesn't have to be an infant." She threw her hands up.

"I'll even take the ones nobody else wants. Give me the sibling group. Shoot. I'll even take one of our clients at the detention center."

Iman looked at Leah, who was looking at her with one eyebrow raised. They both threw their heads back and laughed.

"Okay, okay. I'm overreaching with that one, but you know what I mean."

"Yeah, I think I get it."

"I listen to Maya when she talks about all the cases of child abuse and neglect she's forced to deal with every day from parents who've been blessed to have children. Here I am, I can't even seem to adopt one." Iman closed her eyes and imagined her future family. "I want a house full of kids. At least four. Two of each."

Leah's eyes were filled with curiosity. "Can I get personal?"

"Ask away."

"What exactly is preventing you from having children of your own? With such advance technology at our disposal, what's the problem?"

"I guess it's something I inherited from my mother. I have an abnormally shaped uterus, which can cause problems becoming or remaining pregnant. We've tried in-vitro twice. It was a long shot, but I had to try. I think Micah prayed it didn't work."

"Why would he do that?"

"He was against it from the start. My mother died a few days after giving birth to me and he's afraid the same will happen to me. We've been trying to adopt forever but haven't heard anything."

"You hardly ever talk about your family. Do you normally go home for the holidays?"

Iman shook her head. "I haven't been home since the divorce."

Leah blinked. "Divorce? You've been married before?"

Iman grunted inwardly. This was the reason she didn't like to show vulnerability and get too familiar with her co-workers. It was too easy to allow things to slip. She didn't discuss personal business with anyone other than Micah and Maya.

"I never mentioned that?" She shifted uncomfortably. "It was a long time ago and it didn't last very long." Iman stood and avoided Leah's gaze. "I think I'll just grab a gift card too. I'm ready to get back to work."

She glanced over her shoulder. Leah's expression was difficult to read. Iman wasn't sure if she was shocked or hurt. Choosing to ignore it, she turned and kept walking. She'd revealed more to Leah in the last hour than she'd told her in the four years they'd known each other. She needed to pull herself together. The last thing she wanted was to have co-workers feeling sorry for her. She paid for the card and headed towards the car. She reached into her purse and dug around until she felt one of the pills she kept in the side pocket for easy access. She swallowed it without water. This was going to be a long ride.

Chapter *Three*

Sitting with her seat reclined in her 2016 Mercedes GLC 300 had become Iman's routine since the social worker removed the children from her home. She found that going inside, not hearing arguing or helping them with their homework, was too difficult. When she'd made the decision to take six weeks of leave from work, she hadn't anticipated being home alone. She had plenty of vacation time because she never took off. If the schedules hadn't already been altered, she would have withdrawn her request.

It was probably for the best. The only thing she'd been able to think of lately were her babies. She closed her eyes and smiled.

Kendall, Kaitlyn, and Karlos had become Iman's world. Kendall was a spunky four-year-old, Kaitlyn was a shy thirteen-year-old, and Karlos was fourteen and very protective of his sisters. They were named after their mother, Katrina. She'd gotten into trouble over a guy. Her boyfriend was a big time drug dealer. Some said Katrina was a decent mother and that she'd just had a lapse of judgment when she allowed her boyfriend to talk her into staying home that day because he'd been expecting someone to come by and pick up a package. The day she'd agreed to stay home was the day an undercover cop came in and busted her. She only served a one-year sentence because it was her first offense and they were more interested in the supplier than the dealer. Once Katrina was released, she was able to get her children back. Iman had never met her, but she prayed her babies were in good hands.

Hoping to pass the time, Iman scrolled through her missed calls and emails. As usual, she spent more time deleting and unsubscribing to annoying email users who were bent on sending daily offers. She had two missed calls from their niece, Amari, who'd been calling her a lot lately. Amari and Kaitlyn were around the same age and had many of the same characteristics. Being around her only reminded Iman of what she missed. She made a mental note to call her. Iman looked down at her ringing phone and hit the answer button.

"Hey, Mama," she said into the receiver. Iman listened to her go on and on about why she should be with her family for the holidays.

"It's not all my fault you haven't seen me in five years. I've offered to bring you here on many occasions." Anticipating a long conversation, she connected her phone to the car's Bluetooth speakers.

"Now, don't get me wrong," Vivian continued as if she hadn't heard Iman, "Tina was wrong—"

"Mama, don't. I've told you I don't want to hear her name ever again."

"You need to let that go, Mimi. She probably won't be there anyway. You know she's—"

"You know I love you, Mama, and the last thing I want to do is disrespect you. But, if you're going to keep bringing her up, I'm hanging up."

"Mama," Iman said after she'd gone silent for a long while.

"Fine. I won't bring her name up again. But, I'm worried about you. You can't keep holding on to this stuff. You have to forgive. You hear what I'm saying?"

"Yes, ma'am, I hear you."

"You still going to church?"

"All the time."

"Good."

Iman's phone beeped. Micah's name appeared on the screen. She hit ignore. She wasn't sure why she'd been ignoring his calls. He'd been nothing but supportive through it all. She didn't know how she would've gotten through the miscarriages, fertility treatments, and the failed in-vitro attempts without him. He seemed to care about her more than anything else and she loved him for it. But that wasn't enough for her. Avoidance was better than him trying to make her feel better because the only thing he did was make her feel worse. She hated when people felt sorry for her.

"What's it gone be?" Vivian cut into Iman's thoughts.

"What's that?"

"Are you ready to let go of this mess and spend the holidays with your family? I can see why you may not like Christmas, but you could come around for Thanksgiving."

"You know you can always come here, Mama."

"I don't know. Humph. It's a different kind of cold up there in Maryland. I still don't know why you felt the need to leave the south and move way up there. But, I do want to see you, so we'll see."

Five minutes after they disconnected the call, Iman stared down at her ringing phone. The number wasn't saved in her contacts and the area code didn't look familiar. She sent it to voicemail.

Instead of voicemail, a text came through. *Hey Mimi, it's Tiana. I'm sure I'm the last person you want to hear from. Please call me. It's important.*

Chapter Four

Drenched in sweat, Iman sat up in bed. She struggled to regulate her breathing. She kicked the covers back and sat on the side of her bed, grateful Micah wasn't there to ask questions. *Another bad dream? Wanna talk about it? Maybe you should see someone about that.*

What was it with people always wanting to talk about everything? Talking wouldn't do any good. Talking about it would only keep it alive. She wanted it dead. Buried. Occasionally, that included the person in the dream. But since wishing death on someone was frowned upon among believers, she shook those thoughts from her mind.

After a glance at the clock on the nightstand, Iman was shocked to see that it was 9:22. She couldn't remember the last time she'd slept past seven. Her thoughts had taken up enough of her time. Her vacation had begun and she had things on her agenda to take care of.

After she showered and dressed, Iman made her bed, grabbed her laptop, and pulled up the website to the Center for Surrogacy. She'd already skimmed through the website to learn more about the process.

It took her all of ten minutes to complete the application. "Wow, that was fast," she said after she received an email. She opened the document and read through all fifty pages. She was glad to see they were thorough in learning the background of the surrogate mothers. Her job was easy. The only thing she needed was insurance, money, medical history and to sign a few documents. They even provided pictures of the potential mothers and she was allowed to screen them.

The process would be long and evasive, but she didn't mind, as long as she got what she wanted in the end. This was much better than adoption. She may not be able to carry a baby to term, but her eggs worked fine. She'd mastered forging Micah's signature. Her biggest concern was trying to figure out how to get his sperm. She'd go to the appointments and get all the information needed so she could present a good case to Micah. He'd be upset that she'd gone behind his back but, as always, he'd come around. He'd proven that he loved her and would stick by her no matter what. If this act changed his position, maybe he never loved her.

After looking over the information, Iman called and made the appointment. "Yes, that works for me. I'll see you Wednesday morning at ten."

"Who will you see Wednesday morning at ten?"

Iman almost jumped out of her skin. "Could you not sneak up on me like that? Geez, Micah. You almost scared me to death."

Micah walked into the room. "What are you doing?"

Iman closed all tabs and shut down her laptop. "Nothing much. Just browsing the net. What are you doing here anyway?"

Micah sat down beside Iman. "I don't see my first patient until twelve. You were so out of it this morning; I didn't want to leave you. I had Erica move some appointments around."

Iman stood, walked to the dresser and placed her laptop on top. "You didn't need to do that. I'm fine. I was just a little tired." She grabbed her phone and put her appointment information into her calendar. She felt Micah's intense gaze. "You can go back to work now. I don't need a sitter."

Micah stood next to Iman and leaned against the wall. "I'm not the enemy here, Iman."

"What are you talking about now?"

"This." He threw his hand out to her in an upward motion, scanning her from foot to head. "The body language. The attitude. The silent treatment. What's your problem?"

Iman rolled her eyes. "What do you think the problem is, Micah? You're my problem."

Micah's chest heaved up and down. He breathed in deeply, likely trying to control his tone. "You need to get some help. This whole thing about you wanting a child has become a sick obsession. What do you want me to do about it? We've been married three years and the first two we had sex almost every day of the week. And, it wasn't even that great." He stopped and then closed his eyes and sighed. "I didn't mean it like that."

"Oh, you meant it. You may not have meant to say it, but you meant it."

"What I'm saying is we don't make love. We're just going through the motions. It's like a chore. Afterwards, you lay there with your legs in the air and a pillow underneath your hips to keep my semen in. I don't even think you enjoy it. It shouldn't be that way. It's like you don't care about me, our marriage, or anything else other than having a child."

"I do care about our marriage. I love you. I laid all the cards on the table before you married me. You know how important it is for me to have children and you said you were on board. Whatever it took."

"Of course I was on board. The idea of making babies with you sounded great. What man wouldn't get excited at the thought of lots and lots of sex?"

Iman rolled her eyes and sat on the side of the bed, scrolling through her phone. "Whatever. I've given up the idea of getting pregnant. I let that go months ago."

"Yeah. You were fine as long as Kendall, Kaitlyn, and Karlos were here. But as soon as they left, you became distant. Ignoring my phone calls. Not coming to bed until after I've fallen asleep. We've gone from duty sex to none at all."

"So what? Is that all I am to you? A romp under the sheets?"

"You're twisting my words. You know that's not what I'm saying." Micah looked at his watch. "I'm going to work."

"So, just like that, you're going to leave?"

"What am I here for? You're not ready to work anything out."

Iman folded her arms and leaned against the dresser. "Whatever, Micah. Just don't go getting your feelings all hurt when—"

Micah stopped at the doorway and turned back. "When what?"

"Nothing." Iman straightened and pushed passed him.

"Don't go and do anything crazy." He walked behind her, following her through the hallway, down the stairs, and into the kitchen.

Iman grabbed a water bottle from the fridge and drank half of it. She put the top back on and sat it on the counter. "Don't you have patients to see about? I'm sure you're doing everything to make sure they're happy." Iman walked into the living room and sat on the sofa.

Micah followed her. "Why don't you just say what's on your mind, so I can go?"

"You like to pretend you're doing all you can, but you're not. You won't even consider surrogacy."

Micah grunted. “This again. That’s not normal, Iman. Excuse me for not wanting some other woman carrying my child.”

“Who do you think carried the babies you want to adopt? There’s no difference.”

“That’s not the same and you know it. I’m done arguing with you about this and I’m not changing my mind. We’ve already paid a fortune for fertility treatments and in-vitro. If God wants us to have children, He will make it happen.”

He walked to where Iman sat, leaned down and tried to kiss her, but she turned her head. He kissed her forehead anyway and walked out the door.

Chapter *Five*

"Excuse me, baby. Can you grab that for me?"

Iman looked in the direction of the older lady, who looked to be in her mid to late seventies. She walked over and picked up the bag of store brand cereal she'd dropped and tried to grab with the cane she'd just placed in the basket of the motorized cart she was riding in. After a quick scan of the contents in her basket, Iman saw a bag of pinto beans, corn meal, cereal, milk, and about five store brand canned goods.

"Here you go." Iman handed her the box. "Can I help you with anything else?"

"No, baby. That's it. You go on and finish your shopping."

Iman hesitated but then proceeded to the next aisle to finish her shopping for Thanksgiving dinner. As she walked up and down each aisle, Iman felt compelled to go back and insist on helping the older lady. Her pastor always said whenever you feel a strong urge to do something positive, it's probably the Holy Spirit leading you so don't ignore it.

Iman looked over her shoulder and didn't see her anymore. She walked around, looking up and down several aisles while picking up a few other items on her list. Finally, she headed to check out. Being so close to Thanksgiving Day, she was pleasantly surprised to find an empty register. The young lady rung up her last item just as the older lady rode up in her shopping cart.

Pretending to look for something in her purse, Iman took a few steps forward, enough to give the lady room to check out. She wasn't sure why she stood there fidgeting like a teenager with a crush trying to figure out what to say to a boy. It was probably because when someone told her they didn't want or need her help, she took it to mean they didn't need her help.

"How's it going, Ms. Bessie?" the sales clerk asked the older lady.

"Oh, I'm making it," Ms. Bessie said. "These seventy-four year old knees botherin' me again, but I thank the Lord they still workin'."

"I saw you walk in with your cane. Where's your personal cart today?"

Ms. Bessie smacked her lips and sighed. "I can't find my card nowhere. I looked all over the house for it. You know it won't start without it. But I had to have something to eat and a cab just won't do. Too expensive, you know. So, I just grabbed this here cane and came on down."

Iman took that as her cue to join the conversation. She walked closer to Ms. Bessie and leaned down. "Let me give you a ride."

This time Ms. Bessie didn't protest. "I'm gonna take you up on that offer."

Iman grabbed Ms. Bessie's bags and placed them onto the back seat of her car before putting her own bags in the trunk. Ms. Bessie sat down and immediately started to rub her legs.

"I don't like you walking up and down these streets by yourself like this."

Ms. Bessie gave Iman a warm smile. "Not too many people care about the elderly these days. I appreciate you giving me a ride. Turn right at the first light." She let her body relax a bit. "I don't always have a choice."

"Don't you have any family? Children to take you places?"

"My husband died seven years ago and my two children live too far away. My son tried to get me to move to California with him, but I can't live in such a busy place. I'd rather stay right here in Lutherville where I know how to get around. If I want to go to the city, Baltimore is just a cab ride away."

"Are you from this area?"

"Oh no. I grew up in Alabama. My family migrated up this way when I was fifteen."

"You don't have any church members to take you anywhere?"

Ms. Bessie laughed. "Chile, I ain't gone bother them. These young people have their families to take care of and they work every day. I'm getting old, but I still get around fine. Turn right up in here."

Iman looked around. "Right here?" She realized she had a frown on her face and quickly relaxed her muscles. She didn't want to offend her. The house she lived in looked like it was nice, once upon a time. The grass had grown up around it, bushes covered her front windows, and fifty percent of the paint had come off. There were potholes that needed to be filled and the stairs leading to the front door needed replacing. Something had to be done. It wasn't safe for her to live like this.

"Thanks, baby. I sho' appreciate it."

"Wait." Iman grabbed a notepad and pen from her purse. "Here's my cell and home numbers. Call me anytime you need to go anywhere."

Ms. Bessie smiled. "You married, Emma?" She didn't bother to take the paper.

"It's Iman and, yes ma'am, I am."

"Any children?"

Ms. Bessie must have noticed the solemn look on Iman's face. "Enjoy your husband. Don't be in such a hurry to have children."

She saw the curious look on Iman's face and chuckled. "Now, don't get me wrong. Children are a blessing. But eventually, they grow up and leave. And when they do, it's just the two of you. And sometimes, those grown kids will forget about you. But, that man that God blessed you with, he gon' be there. You trust the God that's in him, listen when he tell ya God will work it out, and you cherish him."

She patted Iman's shoulder and stepped out of the car. She'd gotten the bags out of the backseat and gone inside, when Iman realized she was still sitting there with her mouth hanging open.

Chapter Six

Iman put the rest of the onion and bell peppers into the crockpot, sprinkled some more garlic inside, and put the top back on. Ms. Bessie's words about trusting the God in Micah convicted Iman. She'd been distant with him and he didn't deserve that. To make up for it, she was preparing his favorite meal, pot roast with carrots, potatoes, and onions. She wasn't sure if it was his favorite meal, but it was the only thing she cooked that he seemed to enjoy.

The ringing of the phone caught Iman off guard. Nobody ever called their home phone except telemarketers. She walked over to the kitchen counter and looked at the caller ID where her husband's name was displayed, but it wasn't his number.

"Hello," Iman answered.

"Who is this answering Micah's phone?" The caller yelled into the receiver. "Put Micah on the line right now."

Iman looked at the phone as if it had offended her. God Himself had to have been holding Iman's mouth shut. She took three deep breaths. “I’m Iman. May I ask what the nature of your all is for Micah?”

“This is Solei Carrington. Micah’s wife,” the woman shouted.

Iman rolled her eyes. “That’s where you’re wrong. Because I’m Micah’s wife. Have been for three years. Now, ex-wife, how can I help you?”

Apparently, Solei hadn’t heard that Micah remarried because she paused as if she was letting the revelation sink in. It didn’t take long for her to recover. “Put Micah on the phone.”

“I will do no such thing and you have exactly five seconds to tell—”

“No she did not just hang up on me.” Iman didn’t have time to entertain her foolishness anyway. She had less than an hour to get to church for women’s bible study. Though she was curious as to why, after all this time, Solei finally decided to get in touch with Micah after walking out with no explanation.

“First Tiana, now Solei. Why are these people testing me?”

Iman sent Micah a quick text. *Call me ASAP.*

She wasn’t sure what Ms. Solei had planned, but Iman was not in the mood to be bothered.

Chapter Seven

"What doth it profit, my brethren, though a man say he hath faith, and have not works? Can faith save him?

If a brother or sister be naked, and destitute of daily food,

And one of you say unto them, depart in peace, be ye warmed and filled; notwithstanding ye give them not those things which are needful to the body; what doth it profit?

Even so faith, if it hath not works, is dead, being alone."

Iman didn't bother to look down at her Bible as Jacqueline, the women's ministry leader read the passage. She knew the verses by heart and already had an idea of the direction she was headed.

"We all know the scripture says faith without works is dead," Jacqueline said. "But, we're going to really dig into this for a moment and we're going to put these verses in action over the next few days. I want to challenge each of you to get busy this holiday season. I know it's time for family and friends, but there are some who don't have family or friends. You don't have to spend all day every day with them; just look around and lend a hand, make a difference in someone else's life."

She paused and glanced around at everyone's faces. Nobody seemed to object, so she continued. "Is anyone believing God for anything? Something that seems impossible. Maybe you're dealing with a difficult situation. Have you ever noticed that whenever we're going through something, it's all you can think about? Does it consume your thoughts? Cause anxiety? Lack of sleep? It shouldn't be that way. The Bible says to cast your care upon Him, for He cares for you."

Some of the women responded with amen and some looked at each other with smirks, as if to say *yeah right*.

"I know," Jacqueline continued, "I know sometimes that's easier said than done. But, I've learned through the years once you take your mind off your problems and focus on meeting the needs of others, one of two things happen: you realize your problems are minor in comparison and you begin to be thankful for what you do have, or you realize the problem is still there, but you have peace now because you're letting faith work for you. You see, faith is not about hope. Faith is an action word. You have to do something."

She turned her attention to the table in the corner and pointed. "I want everyone to grab a partner." Many of the ladies turned and started chatting.

"Wait. Wait." Jacqueline raised her hands to get everyone's attention. "Before you move, I want everyone to come up and grab a gratitude jar."

"A what?" One of the ladies yelled.

"Each day, you and your family are to write down one thing you're grateful for and put it inside the jar. This is to help start the day thinking on positive things, rather than negative. Do this each day and watch how much better your day flows."

"Ok, girl," Maya, who was sitting next to Iman, said. "What are we going to do?"

It was a given that they'd team up. The two had been inseparable ever since Iman joined Agape Christian Fellowship almost six years ago. She'd joined shortly after her divorce was final. Maya was assigned as her prayer partner and the two connected right away.

Iman looked down at her vibrating phone. Micah was calling. "Give me a minute." She stepped out into the foyer and answered, quickly relaying her earlier conversation with his ex-wife. He was as shocked as she was about the call from Solei. "You have no idea why she's calling?"

"No. And I'm not interested in hearing anything she has to say. She's a little late for that," he said.

Micah told Iman he'd extended his hours to accommodate a few of his patients. That wasn't unusual for him. He did everything he could to assure his patients and their families were treated and well informed.

To the average person, Micah sounded calm, but knowing his ex was trying to reach him had changed his mood.

"I'm sorry, baby," Iman said. "I shouldn't have told you about this while you're working. I should have waited until you were home."

"It's fine," he said. "Glad to hear from you. You've been kind of distant these last few days. You sound better."

"I am. I'm in church right now. I'll probably grab lunch with Maya."

"Oh, before I forget," Micah said. "Hannah says Amari has been trying to reach you. She misses you. She wants to stay with us during their Thanksgiving and winter break."

"That's fine. What about Hannah? Will she be joining us?"

"No. She said she needed to catch up on some housework. She's always been kind of a loner. We can send her a plate."

A few moments of awkward silence passed before Iman spoke again, "Are you going to return Solei's call?"

"I hadn't planned to."

She waited for something more but realized he was done talking about it. "Okay. Well, I'll see you when you get home. I put a pot roast in the crock pot."

"Really?"

Iman dropped her head. She could imagine his eyebrows raised and a slight smirk in the corner of his lips. She hadn't cooked since the kids were taken out of their home. "I'm sorry. I have to do better."

"What time should we come over for Thanksgiving dinner?" Maya asked after the waitress left with their order.

"Come over Wednesday. We can cook together. Amari will be there. You know how she loves competing with Tyler on those video games. I'm sure Micah won't mind. It'll give him the perfect excuse to shut up in his man cave and watch sports all night."

"Sounds like fun. I can come as early as you want. I have the week off."

"Anytime after one is good. I have an appointment at ten."

"What kind of appointment? Everything alright?"

Iman waved her hands. "No. Nothing like that. Everything's fine. I need to take care of some things."

Maya was her closest friend, but she and Micah were like family. She wasn't ready to tell her plans yet, not even to Maya.

"Do you have any ideas for our faith in action challenge?" Iman asked.

She looked at Iman suspiciously before responding. "I volunteer at Damascus Community Outreach every year and help feed the needy the day before and the morning of Thanksgiving and a few times a week during the month of December. You should join me this year."

"Am I the only person that doesn't volunteer during the holidays? Leah mentioned a few days ago that she does the same thing. I'm fine with that. I'll bring Amari with me. She's been asking for us to do something together for weeks."

Iman looked down at her phone and groaned.

"What was that about?" Maya asked.

"Just another email address about to go to spam."

"Care to elaborate?" Maya asked.

The waitress sat their drinks down. Iman took a sip of her lemonade before she spoke, "Tiana."

Maya's eyes grew wide. She was the only person in Iman's life, besides Micah, who was privy to the Tiana drama. "What did she say?"

"Don't know. Don't care. I'm ignoring it; the same way I've been ignoring her calls."

"When did she call?"

"Earlier in the week, followed with a text. When she called again yesterday, I blocked her number. I'm about to send her emails to spam. How does she keep finding my information?"

"You're not curious?"

"Couldn't care less." The food came. Iman said grace and started eating right away. Maya must have taken the hint that Iman was done with talk of Tiana. "By the way," Iman said. "Solei called."

Iman picked the wrong time to blurt that out because Maya went into a coughing fit at the mention of her name. "She's got a lot of nerve calling after all this time," she finally said.

Maya grew up with Micah and his siblings. Her foster mom was good friends with Micah's mother before she passed, so she witnessed firsthand how Solei treated Micah. Not long after Micah and Solei were married, his sister, Hannah, became ill. With no other family around, Micah became her caregiver. He took leave from work and took her to every appointment. He also took care of her daughter, Amari. After about two months of not being the center of Micah's attention, Solei packed her bags, wiped out their joint accounts, and left without so much as leaving a note.

"I never liked her," Maya said. "I told him from the beginning she was no good for him. She acted as if the world owed her something and she looked at his family and friends as if we were beneath her. What did she want?" Maya's eyes squinted and her nose flared.

"Calm down, girl. It was only a phone call."

She put her fork down. "I'm not even hungry anymore."

Iman chuckled. "Let's wait and find out why she's calling before we get worked up."

"I can't stop thinking about how bad Hannah felt after she left. To this day, she blames herself for their marriage ending." Maya looked at Iman and smiled. "I guess I shouldn't hate her too much. Had she not left, you two wouldn't be together."

"That's true."

"Is your mom finally coming this year?" Maya asked, changing the subject.

Iman poked out her lips and looked at Maya out the corner of her eye. "I seriously doubt it. I invite her every year and she never comes."

"Troopers arrest two for multiple Eureka County robberies."

"This is why I don't watch the news." Iman scooted closer to Micah and laid her head on his chest. "If someone isn't blowing up something or murdering someone, they're robbing people."

Watching the ten o'clock news was a ritual to Micah. "It's important to know what's happening in the world," he said.

"But do we have to hear about it before bed? It makes me have bad dreams."

"You say that every night. I've seen you wake up in a cold sweat, but something tells me it has nothing to do with the ten o'clock news."

"Hush up and kiss me, man."

"You don't have to tell me twice."

One Wish

Iman grabbed the remote and turned off the TV. She straddled his thighs, and teased him with kisses up and down his chest and neck. It was time she showed her husband just how much he meant to her. After tomorrow, she hoped he remembered this feeling.

Chapter *Eight*

"Not today," Iman yawned.

She threw on her black satin robe and ran downstairs to answer the ringing phone. It was too early in the morning to deal with more foolishness. If the person calling was Tiana or Solei, she would threaten them both with a restraining order.

Looking at the caller ID, Iman wasn't sure how to feel. The caller ID read Faith and Hope Adoption Agency. Was this the call she'd been waiting years for? After being let down so much, she wasn't sure if she should feel excitement or dread. Instead of trying to figure it out, she answered the phone.

The phone receiver still in her hand, Iman sat back into the chair and let it sink in. Words she'd wanted to hear for so long. A few weeks was a little too close to Christmas for comfort. She wondered if she should decline and hope for another call after the New Year. After all, this was her and it was the end of November. Too close to Christmas and too close to her birthday.

Placing the receiver on the counter, Iman went upstairs to find her cell. She wanted to share the news with Micah. He didn't keep his phone on him when he was with patients and she didn't know his work number from memory.

"Where is my phone?" Iman did a quick scan over her bedroom. She looked underneath the bed, behind the nightstand and didn't see it. She sat on the side of the bed and retraced her steps from the night before. She went into the bathroom and saw Micah's phone on the sink. "He must have taken my phone by mistake." Iman proceeded to turn on the shower and begin her day.

"Oh no!" Iman panicked. "Micah has my phone. Why did we have to get identical phones?" She took a quick shower. With no time to straighten her hair, she opted for a wash-n-go and pulled it back into a puff with a black elastic headband.

Glad she'd taken time to get her clothes together the night before, she grabbed the slacks and sweater from her walk-in closet, put it on, stepped into her boots and grabbed her leather jacket.

She sped down the street, in hopes of getting her phone before Micah saw the appointment alert that popped up an hour before every appointment she put in her calendar.

Not wanting to risk wasting any more time trying to find a place to park in the garage, she parked on the street, put money in the meter and ran inside.

"Haven't seen you around lately, Mrs. Carrington. How are you?" Erica, Micah's secretary stood and greeted Iman as she entered. Iman gave a polite smile and embraced the woman she'd grown fond of.

"Been super busy. Is Micah around?"

"I think he's with a patient, but you can wait in his office if you like." She reached in her drawer. "Take this key in case it's locked."

"Thanks, Erica."

Iman smiled and waved, as the many nurses she'd become familiar with greeted her. There were a few new faces. One in particular stood back watching Iman with interest. Her uniform was about two sizes too small and her cleavage was screaming to bust out. She couldn't have been any older than twenty-three or twenty-four. Iman didn't have time to entertain her or figure out if she knew her or not. She was on a mission.

She turned the corner that led to Micah's office and went inside. His desk was locked. *Just my luck.* She saw his coat hanging up and prayed her phone was in the pocket.

She felt inside both side pockets and didn't find it. She remained hopeful and kept feeling around for it. Lo and behold, it was in the inner pocket. She took it out, put it in her purse, and retrieved his phone. As she was about to place it in his jacket, the door opened.

"I've been expecting you."

Iman's heart pounded so loudly, it wouldn't have surprised her if he could hear it. She looked at the time. Her appointment wasn't for an hour and a half so the alert hadn't come up. She decided to play it cool.

"Expecting me?" She raised her eyebrows. "Why?"

The corners of his lips turned up. "Did Ms. Matthews not call you?"

"Oh my goodness," she squeaked. "Yes." Iman wasn't sure if the excitement was sinking in from the phone call or if it was because she hadn't been caught.

Micah walked up to her and she fell into his arms. The mix-up with the phones caused her to forget what could be the best news she'd heard in years.

"Can you believe it? In two weeks, we're going to have a baby girl."

"I can believe it," he said. "I told you to wait and let God do it. He always comes through, doesn't He?"

Ms. Bessie was right. I should've not only trusted God but also the God in Micah. He really was trying. I'd better get my attitude in check towards Micah before I lose him.

"Did she tell you what happened?" Micah asked.

"Yes. She said a fifteen-year-old runaway came in wanting to give her baby up. She wants to go back home, but she knew her mother wouldn't let her come back if she was pregnant. Somehow our papers got lost in the archives.

She said once we updated a few days ago, she received an alert and our name was next on the list."

Iman looked at Micah suspiciously. "But, I didn't update our information."

He smiled. "I did."

"When?"

"The day the social worker came for the kids. You were so hurt. I had to do something."

"I love you so much right now," Iman said. "I could take you right here on this desk."

He laughed. "If I didn't have an appointment in two minutes, I'd let you. Can I get a rain check?"

Iman pulled Micah's head down and gave him a passionate kiss. "Let that hold you until later."

Once he was out of the office, Iman pulled the door up and sat down behind his desk. She scrolled through her contacts until she came to the Center for Surrogacy. She called and cancelled the meeting.

"You didn't trust me."

Iman gasped at the sound of Micah's voice.

"You made an appointment to meet with surrogates? I can't believe you went behind my back."

The hurt in his voice caused her throat to tighten. She'd been caught. Unable to form words, Iman stared at him with her mouth open.

He walked to his desk and grabbed a file he must have forgotten.

"Micah, I—"

He put one hand up to stop her. "Don't." Disappointment stamped across his face. He held Iman's gaze a few seconds and then turned and walked out of the office.

Iman squeezed her eyes shut and inhaled deeply and repeated. Finally she stood, walked out of his office, and locked the door. She gave the key back to Erica and saw Micah from the corner of her eye. She spotted him at the end of the hall talking with the new nurse that had stared at Iman earlier. She placed her hand on his arm when she spoke. She acted too familiar, in Iman's opinion.

Micah looked in Iman's direction and held her gaze. The nurse followed his gaze and smiled. Still watching Iman, her hand slid slowly down his arm. He turned his attention back to the nurse, without bothering to remove her hand from his body.

Erica watched the exchange. Iman turned her attention to Erica. "What's her name?"

"Candi."

"Figures."

"Is she new?"

"Yes and she's as ditzy as they come. I know what you're thinking. Don't. You have absolutely nothing to worry about. Trust. But, I'll keep my eye out, just in case." Erica walked around to her desk and sat in her chair. "But if I were you, I'd make an appearance more often. You know, to make your presence known."

Iman watched the pair until they disappeared into the exam room. "Here." She pulled up her contacts and handed Erica her phone. “Put your number in. I think we need to stay in touch.”

Chapter *Nine*

"Do you always have a turn out this big?" Iman asked Roger, the coordinator for Damascus community outreach.

"Unfortunately, yes," he said. "In addition to not having enough homeless shelters in the area, people are in need of food. If we didn't feed them on weekdays, many wouldn't eat. Some go all weekend without food."

It was hard to believe a city this size was full of hunger and homelessness. Iman inwardly chided herself. Jacqueline was right. There were people with far more problems than she had and she had the nerve to go behind Micah's back and treat him like he was the enemy. He hadn't spoken to her since the incident in his office. She'd hardly seen him. He'd get off work and go to the gym or visit his cousins and wouldn't come home until after she was already asleep. She'd awakened this morning and noticed that his side of the bed hadn't been slept in.

She'd caught him on his way out. He was behaving suspiciously. Talking on his phone when she'd entered the kitchen but ended the call abruptly when he saw her. He told her he'd see her later and left. He had the day off, so she wondered where he could be going. She didn't dare ask. The part that bothered her most, for the first time since they'd been married, he walked out of the door and didn't kiss her goodbye.

"Hey, Emma."

Iman looked up to see Ms. Bessie coming from the back. "Hi, Ms. Bessie." They embraced. "It's Iman. Good seeing you again."

"I'm not surprised to see you here. I could tell right away you had a good heart."

"Me?" Iman pointed to herself. *Looking at my recent track record, she can't be talking about me.*

"Now, why you lookin' like that? I said you had a good heart. I didn't say you was perfect." She chuckled. "Come on over here with me. Help me with some of these pies."

"You're here working?"

"I try to get up here as much as I can and help cook. You know these youngins don't know what to do."

"I don't know, Ms. Bessie. I can cook a mean sweet potato pie."

"Well, you just let me be the judge of that."

Amari walked up and placed a box of sodas on the floor next to the other boxes many of the volunteers had brought inside from the truck. She linked her arm through Iman's arm. "Are you going in the back to cook? Can I help?" she asked, looking into Iman's eyes.

"No, sweetie." Iman slipped her arm from Amari's and patted her back. "Why don't you see if Leah needs help serving? I'll come back out and check on you in a few."

"Yes, ma'am." Amari slumped her shoulders and did as she was told.

Iman followed Ms. Bessie to the back into the kitchen. "Looks like you got more spring in your step than you did last week."

"Oh yeah. You caught me on a bad day. I'd tripped and almost fell coming down my stairs a few weeks ago. Just needed a little rest and some ice packs on my knee and I'm as good as new."

"You mean you didn't go to the doctor?"

"No, chile." She handed Iman an apron and showed her where the ingredients were. "I can count on one hand how many times I've been to a doctor. I didn't even go to the hospital to have my chirren'. My sister delivered both of them at my house."

She laughed when she saw Iman's shocked expression. "I can see you're worried about me. I saw it the other day. But, believe me, I'm fine. God takes good care of me."

Iman grabbed a measuring cup and started adding the sugar, butter, and eggs to the pot of pre-boiled sweet potatoes on the stove. She stole a glance at Ms. Bessie, who was humming a hymn and moving around the kitchen as if she owned it.

"Now, why are you standing there lookin' at me like that?"

"I'm in awe."

"Is that right?"

"Yes, ma'am. Look at you. I mean, how do you do it?"

"Do what?"

"Stay in such good spirits."

"It's called faith, honey." She grabbed the spoon from Iman's hand and stirred the sweet potato mixture, as if she wasn't doing it right. "I've lived a long time and have had way more problems than what you saw at my house the other day. I'm almost seventy-five years old. I've outlived all seven of my siblings, a few nieces and nephews, and a husband. My daughter won't half talk to me, which means I don't get to see my grandbabies, my son lives thousands of miles away, but he sends me money every month, though I tell him he don't have to. That could've broke me, but it didn't. I look around at all these people here that's hungry. I've never missed a meal. The meal might just be beans and cornbread, but I always eat."

"Iman." Maya came in out of breath. "There you are." She looked around the room and then back to Iman and frowned slightly. "What are you doing back here? Come with me. You've got to see this."

She grabbed Iman's arm and pulled her out into the cafeteria where two TV's were showing the news. It was a continuation of the arrests that were made in Eureka County, Nevada.

There was video footage of a couple being arrested and next to it was a mug shot of the woman involved.

Iman shrugged. "I saw this story the other night. So what?"

"I saw it too," Maya said. "But, this is the first time they showed their faces."

"Should I know them?"

She looked at Iman as if she had two heads.

"What?" Iman asked absently.

"Oh. You didn't meet her, did you?"

"Meet who?"

"That's Solei. Micah's ex-wife."

She watched Iman's features change until the light switch came on. "Oh, wow. Seriously?"

"Yep. And based on all the charges, she'll be locked away for a long time."

"Wonder if that's why she called."

"But why would she call you guys for that?"

Iman shrugged. "Maybe she needed an alibi."

"Or some bail money," Maya said.

Iman studied Solei's features. Tall, slim, light skin tone, long straight hair with blonde highlights. A complete opposite of Iman, who was 5'5, dark skinned, with short black hair. She noted Solei's nose ring and a tattoo of a scorpion on her neck. She was attractive but had an edginess about her. "She seems a little hood for Micah's taste, if you ask me. Wonder if Micah has seen this."

"Call and ask."

"We're not on the best of terms right now."

Maya took her attention from the television and focused on Iman. “What’s going on?”

“Iman Carrington?” Iman turned in the direction of the unfamiliar male voice.

“Yes, I’m Iman.”

“Someone’s outside asking for you.”

Iman looked at Maya, who was concerned as she was.

“There’s no need for you to look at me like that. ‘Cause I’m coming with you,” she said.

Iman looked up to see Leah, who was sitting and mingling with everyone, looking in their direction. She must have noticed their startled expression. *She doesn’t miss anything. Must be a gift.* Iman smiled and gave her a thumbs up, letting her know everything was fine.

Maya and Iman walked to the door and looked around but didn’t see anyone. They stepped out onto the sidewalk. Iman looked to her immediate right and came face to face with the one person she hadn’t seen in almost seven years.

“Hey Mi—”

The scowl on Iman’s face must have caused her to think twice before calling her by her nickname because she took two steps back and corrected herself.

“Hi, Iman. Can we talk?”

Chapter Ten

"How did she know where to find me?" Iman paced back and forth across the kitchen floor of her home, while Maya sat back and listened. "If I wanted to be near her, I wouldn't have moved and put three states between us six years ago. Does she not realize how much I detest her? I can't—"

"Detest? That sounds like a fancy word for hate and I know I raised you better than that."

Iman looked up to see her grandma coming down the stairs. "Mama." She ran into her arms. She didn't realize how much she'd missed her until this very moment. "What are you doing here?"

"My son here," she nodded towards Micah, who'd just appeared from the family room, "booked my flight and picked me up early this morning. If not for that FaceTime stuff on this here phone you sent me, I wouldn't have know'd his face, you know, since I didn't get invited to the wedding and you ain't bothered to bring him to meet ya family." She stopped and gave Iman a look of disapproval. "We wanted to surprise you."

Iman made the mistake of looking in Micah's direction. His cold gaze made her shiver. She felt small. While she was accusing him of doing something wrong, as usual, he was thinking about her, while she only thought of herself. She switched her attention to Vivian, whose eyes darted back and forth between Iman and Micah.

"We didn't have a wedding, Mama. We eloped."

Vivian nodded towards Maya. "I bet your friend here was there."

"I'll let you ladies catch up. I'm going to watch the game." Micah turned and left the room.

"I'll ask about that later," Vivian said, once Micah's figure disappeared. "I want to know what all the commotion was about. Who is it that you hate?"

Iman turned, walked to the refrigerator and took out a water bottle. "Your niece. Who else?"

"Oh. She came to see you? What'd she say?"

Vivian must've noticed Iman's careful examination of her face because she started moving around pots and pans, placing them on the stove, opening and closing the refrigerator, as if she was searching for something.

"Mama. What are you doing?"

"Getting ready to start dinner."

Iman looked down at her watch. "It's almost three o'clock. We're eating in two hours. Maya and I cooked most of the food last night and what we didn't cook, Ms. Wanda is bringing."

Vivian looked up for a brief second. "Who is Ms. Wanda?"

"Maya's mom."

"Humph." She started moving again, as if she hadn't heard her. Iman closed their distance and touched her on both shoulders. "Mama. What's going on? Why are you acting nervous?"

She just stood and stared at Iman. "You're scaring me," Iman said. "What's going on?"

Finally, Vivian stopped moving and pulled out a chair and sat at the table. She patted the seat for Iman to sit beside her. Maya excused herself and went to check on Tyler and Amari.

"Don't be upset," she started. "I'm the one that encouraged Tina to reach out to you."

Iman jumped up from her seat. "You had no right. I've told you over and over that I want nothing to do with her. You saw what she did to me. And purposely flaunted it in my face. She wanted me to catch them. You should've saw the smug look she gave me. And I haven't heard from her in all these years. Why now? No thank you. She can save it."

"Are you finished?" Vivian said calmly, as if Iman wasn't ranting only seconds earlier.

"No!" Iman yelled. "How is it that you can make everybody feel so loved and comforted, but when I need you, you aren't here? All this time I've lived here and you never visited. Now, you decide to come when you want to do something for her. You can't be serious." Iman wasn't sure where the tears came from, but they started to flow uncontrollably. "You're the only mom I've ever known and when everything happened, you didn't even come and find me. Sure, you call often. But, you never once came to see how I was doing. But when Tiana, who has a mother, needs you to talk to me, you come running. No!" Iman yelled. "I'm not going to listen to her and I'm done listening to you."

She turned to walk out of the room when Micah ran in with the phone in hand. "We need to get to the hospital. Destiny has had the baby."

Chapter *Eleven*

It'd been less than forty eight hours since the adoption agency called and Iman hadn't had time to adjust to the news. She had her doubts about going through with it, only because the mother was still alive. After going through one disappointment after another, her optimism was fading and she knew it was possible for Destiny to change her mind and keep her baby. She'd heard plenty of cases where that had happened, even after the adoption had gone through. The courts tended to favor the biological parents. She had that possibility on her brain.

"This was unexpected. I thought we at least had a few more weeks to prepare." Iman turned to Micah, who kept his eyes glued to the road.

In the years they'd been married, she never experienced this side of him. The twenty minutes it would take to get to the hospital was enough to make her nerves go haywire. Micah's disinterest in conversing with her only made it worse.

"You're going to sit there and act like I'm not here?"

"Why the sudden interest in talking to me now?" Micah continued to stare straight ahead. "You're the expert at figuring things out on your own."

He parked, stepped out of the car and closed his door. Iman waited for him to come around to her side and open her door. When she saw he wasn't coming, she opened the door and stepped out. "Thanks for getting my door."

"You're good at doing things for yourself these days. You don't need me."

"Real mature, Micah."

She reached out to take hold of his hand, but he placed them in his pocket. Iman stopped walking and glared at him. He didn't notice she'd stopped walking until he reached the door a few feet away. He held the door open and looked back. "Are you coming?"

She kept her feet planted in the same spot with her hands on her hips. She refused to meet her daughter when her husband wasn't speaking to her.

He looked upward and walked back until he stood only a few inches away from her. "I don't have time for your little tantrums. You're the one who's so eager to have a child. Now's your moment. Let's go."

She put her hand on his arm. He didn't flinch. "How long are you going to punish me, Micah? I said I was sorry."

"No," He shook his head. "Actually, you didn't."

"You know me. You know I didn't mean to hurt you. I was just trying to—"

"What?" he interrupted. "Be in control as usual? This desire of yours to have a child has reached an all-time low. You'll do anything to get it, no matter who it hurts. I'm done going through all these changes with you Iman. I—"

"You're what?" She pulled her hand away. "Gonna leave?" A tear streaked down her face. "You're done with me? Fine. Leave, Micah, just like everyone else in my life. Soon enough, I'll have someone that won't hurt me." Iman briskly walked past him and shoved him with the side of her body. Of course, his six foot, one hundred seventy pounds of chiseled muscle didn't budge. Instead, he reached out and pulled her to him and released a long sigh. She laid her head on his chest and choked back a whimper.

"Why do you always go there? I'm not leaving you and I don't plan to let you go either." He lifted her chin with his thumb and looked into her eyes. "I was going to say I don't feel you give me the respect I deserve and that has to change."

She wiped her eyes on his shirt and turned away from him. She reached into her pocket and grabbed a Valium and swallowed it without water.

"Let's put this conversation on hold." He wiped her tears with his thumb. "Let's go inside and meet our little princess."

They interlocked their fingers together and headed towards the hospital entrance. Micah stopped and turned to her before he opened the door.

"What is it?"

"Don't you think you were a bit harsh with Mama Vi earlier?"

Iman dropped her head and sighed. "I know. I didn't realize all of that was in me. I'll make it right when we get home."

He kept his gaze on her. "I said I'll make it right."

Micah shook his head. "That's not it." He reached out with his free hand and opened his palm. "The pills."

She gave him a look of defiance.

"I don't need you to become dependent on these. If you start facing your problems head on, instead of ignoring them, you won't need them."

Reluctantly, Iman reached inside her purse and handed him the pill bottle. He shook his head. "You pulled that pill from your pocket."

She blew out a long breath and reached into her pocket and handed him the Ziploc bag with the rest of the pills.

He put them in his pocket, opened the door, and they walked inside.

In their haste to get to the hospital, they forgot to grab a gift from the nursery. They stopped by the gift shop on their way to Destiny's room to get a teddy bear, balloons and a flower for Destiny.

They passed by an older couple talking loudly and acting every bit ghetto, arguing with the nurse about letting her in to see her daughter who'd just given birth. Iman shook her head and avoided eye contact.

They stopped outside of the door that read 214 and knocked.

"You must be the parents to be?" One of the nurses asked.

Iman smiled and nodded. Destiny was lying down with her head towards the wall facing away from the nurse who was cleaning a screaming baby. "How are you?" Iman asked.

Destiny gave a weak smile and looked at one of the nurses. She then nodded her head in the direction of the baby. "Can you take them somewhere else and do that?"

Micah and Iman looked at each other and then at the nurse. "You don't want to see her?" One of the nurses asked.

"No." Destiny shook her head. "We agreed you would take her as soon as she was born and I requested to not meet them either." She nodded her head towards Micah and Iman.

The nurse finished cleaning the baby and bundled her up. She cut her eyes at Micah and Iman and scooped up the baby. "I'm Linda," she said and headed towards the door. "You can follow me."

Iman looked at Micah with tears in her eyes. "She's so small. Will she be okay?"

"She was born a little early, yes. But her weight is up just enough to where we believe she'll be fine. Had she been a full-term baby, she would've been quite large. Dr. Rudolph examined her and she's very healthy."

"May I?" Iman said to the nurse as soon as they entered the other room.

She looked up and smiled. "You can put that on and there's some sanitizer." She pointed to the gown hanging in the corner of the room.

"Of course." Iman threw on the gown and cleaned her hands.

She made herself comfortable in a rocker and rocked her baby for the first time. "My baby." She couldn't believe it had finally happened.

"She's so tiny." Iman stared down at her pale skin and continued rocking.

"She's perfect." Micah walked over to where his girls sat and pulled the cover back that hid her face. "Hi, princess."

She blinked her eyes rapidly until they opened. Her eyes were trained on Micah, as if he was the only person in the room.

They couldn't take their eyes off her.

"Would you like to feed her?"

They'd forgotten the nurse was in the room. She walked over and handed Iman a one-ounce bottle. It was the most beautiful thing she'd ever seen.

"What are you going to name her?" Linda asked.

"With all that's been going on, we haven't even discussed a name," Micah said.

"How about Alyssa?" Iman said.

"Alyssa it is." Micah kissed Iman's forehead. His eyes beamed with pride, as if he'd produced her himself.

"I'll give you guys a few moments alone with her. I'll be back in about five minutes." Linda excused herself from the room.

"I can't wait until her nursery is set up," Iman said.

"Everything happened so quickly. We haven't had time to go shopping yet."

"All taken care of," Iman said, while still smiling down at Alyssa. "I've ordered everything already. It will be delivered this Saturday."

"Of course you did." Micah stepped away from Iman and Alyssa and leaned against the wall. "Hopefully, I'll at least have the opportunity to put the crib together."

"Why would I keep you from putting a crib together?" Iman finally looked up, realizing something was bothering Micah.

"Never mind." Micah stood up straight. "I need to make a phone call." Micah headed towards the door.

"What is it now?" Iman asked.

Micah didn't bother to look back or respond. Very calmly, he left the room.

Alyssa started to squirm in Iman's arms. Iman had always heard babies could sense tension. Based on the reaction she was getting from Alyssa, she was beginning to believe it had some merit to it. Alyssa may be small, but her lungs worked perfectly fine.

Iman lifted her upright and rubbed her back. "I'm sorry, princess. Mommy has been upsetting Daddy a lot lately, but I promise it won't always be this way. Mommy's going to do better by Daddy. I'm going to do everything I can to make sure you have a happy and carefree childhood."

Alyssa let out a loud burp and milk spewed from her mouth and nose. Her eyes glazed and she gasped for air.

Immediately, Iman pushed the call button and asked for a nurse. Too worried to wait, she headed to the door and went out into the hall to get help. Two nurses met her as soon as she opened the door. They took Alyssa from her arms, rushed down the hall and went into a room.

The tears in Iman's eyes blinded her, as her body rested against a nearby table. "What's wrong with her? Will she be okay?" she asked with a shaky voice.

"Baby, what's wrong?" Micah put his phone in his jacket pocket and rushed to Iman's side.

She fell into his arms and mumbled an incoherent sentence. Micah looked to the nurse for an answer.

"I'm sure everything will be fine. The baby started choking. This happens more than you think."

Iman gasped for air and spoke in between sobs. "I. Almost. Killed. Our. Baby." She sniffed. "I'm a terrible mother. I didn't know what to do."

"I'm sure you didn't do anything wrong," Micah said. "This is your first time with a newborn. You heard the nurse. It's common." He rubbed his hands up and down her arms and walked her back into the room.

Once he got her into a chair and calmed down, he poured her a cup of ice water from a table in the corner of the room.

She closed her eyes and rested her head against the back of the chair. She inhaled and exhaled slowly, looking at Micah who leaned against the wall watching her. "I'm sorry."

Micah's eyebrows dipped. "Baby, you didn't do anything wrong."

Iman shook her head. "Not about that." She handed him the empty cup and waited for him to set it on the table. He sat on the side of the bed and took her hand in his. "For making you feel disrespected and not including you in important things and for going behind your back all those times. I get it. I was wrong."

Micah kneeled in front of Iman and took both her hands into his. He kissed the back of each and then looked into her eyes.

"What was that for?" she asked.

"This is the first time since I've known you that you've acknowledged you were wrong and apologized."

Iman's forehead crinkled and she opened her mouth to protest. "I've apologized—"

He cut her off by placing his mouth over hers in a kiss. At that moment, the anxiety she'd felt minutes ago, dissipated.

There was a knock at the door. Iman stood abruptly, almost knocking Micah over. "Is Aly okay?" Iman asked as soon as Linda walked inside. "Where is she?"

"She's fine, but we want to keep a close watch on her."

Iman looked from Linda to Micah and back to Linda again. "Did I do something wrong?"

"Absolutely not," Linda reassured her. "You did everything right by getting help right away. This happens often with premature babies. It's a good thing this happened. It might have saved her life."

Micah's head snapped in Linda's direction. "What do you mean?"

"I-I-I'm sorry," Linda stammered. "I've said too much. Dr. Rudolph will be in shortly to explain everything."

"Will she be okay?" Tears welled up in Iman's eyes. Linda offered a polite smile and walked out of the room.

Iman opened the door and walked with quick steps to catch up with her. She reached her, grabbed her arm and turned her around.

Linda's eyes bucked. "Get your hands off me." Iman had used more force than she'd meant to.

"Not until you explain to me what's going on. You can't tell me something like that and leave."

"Iman." Micah ran up and grabbed his wife. "You have to calm down." He looked at Linda, who surprisingly had a look of compassion. "I'm sorry about this."

She nodded and then turned the corner and went into a room.

"You're need to get control over your emotions before I end up having to bail you out of jail."

"Look, there's the doctor." Iman moved from Micah's hold and approached Dr. Rudolph. "How is she?"

"Let's talk in the room." He said.

They went back inside the room. Dr. Rudolph began talking right away. As roused up as Iman was, she was glad he got straight to the point because if she had to wait any longer, she was sure to have a heart attack right there.

"Her temperature has dropped and we've placed her in an incubator."

"But, I thought she was okay."

"She weighs a little more than five pounds, which is a decent amount of weight for a newborn, but she could use a few weeks for her lungs to mature. Unfortunately, because she was almost an entire month early, there are still precautions we have to take. Her temperature should be up in no time. She's in good hands." He waited to see if they had any questions. When they didn't say anything, he continued. "We found that her lungs lack surfactant."

"What's that?" Iman asked.

"It's a substance that allows the lungs to expand and can cause respiratory distress syndrome because the lungs can't expand and contract normally."

Iman sucked in a breath, and Micah put his arm around her and pulled her close to him.

"I know this sounds like a lot, but believe me, this is very common among premature births and we've had many success stories. She will have to stay in the nursery for the duration of her stay, but you are more than welcome to visit anytime."

Chapter *Twelve*

"This is too cute." Iman held up a hot pink onesie with a navy and white cupcake and a pair of navy and white polka dot pants with a hot pink cupcake on the backside and grinned widely.

Maya shook her head and smiled. "You do realize you're going to have to return half of this stuff, right?"

Iman frowned. "Why?"

"Aly won't be this size long. You need to spread out the sizes."

"The bigger sizes aren't as adorable." Iman placed the items into the cart without a second thought.

"I'm excited for you. This couldn't have happened to a better person. Have you completed the nursery yet?"

Iman's eyes beamed and the corners of her lips turned up. "Yes. Finished it yesterday. I didn't tell you?" Iman looked down at her phone and sighed. She put her phone in the back pocket of her jeans and started back browsing.

"Tiana again?"

"Who else? I blocked her number. Now, she's emailing. After all this time, I don't know why she's so interested in speaking with me."

"Maybe you should've stayed and heard her out. If you hadn't walked away, this could've been over by now."

"Let's get a few more diapers and I'll be ready to check out." Iman didn't feel the need to respond because she had no plans of speaking to her backstabbing cousin ever again.

Iman had been to the hospital every day for the past week. Today was the day they would bring baby Alyssa home and she refused to ruin it by discussing Tiana. She had just enough time to drop her purchases at home and head to the hospital.

Iman had purchased so many baby items she needed two shopping carts. The items totaled over $700 and that only included diapers, wipes, a few other essentials and clothing.

"What?" Iman said after she glanced at Maya, who stood there shaking her head from side to side. "The car seat and stroller was expensive. I had to have it."

Maya lifted her hands and smiled. "I didn't say a word."

Maya walked into the nursery, stopped in the middle of the floor and did a complete turn.

The walls were painted in two different shades of pink. The carpet and rocker was beige. The curtains were pink and white. There was a white crib with big brown bows across the front. A gold crown on the wall in the center of the crib with white Chiffon coming from the center. Directly above Maya's head was a white chandelier.

"This room is fit for a queen," Maya said. She did another scan of the room and wrinkled her forehead. "Why does this nursery look familiar?"

Iman laughed. "I wondered if you would notice. This is almost a replica of Tamera Mowry-Housley's baby room."

Maya snapped her finger. "Of course. How could I have forgotten?" Maya and Iman shared a love for 90's sitcoms. There had been times where they'd spent their entire Saturday binge watching Sister Sister reruns. And when the sisters had their own reality show, they never missed an episode. When Iman saw Tamera's Instagram post showing her baby's nursery, she said when she had her little girl, hers would be similar.

Maya moved to the far side of the room. She opened the closet and cut her eye towards Iman. "The closet is full." She pointed to the bags of clothing she and Iman had brought upstairs. "Where do you plan to put all of these things?"

"I guess I got a little carried away."

"Just a little," Maya said.

Iman blasted praise music as she drove down the interstate towards the hospital. She was on top of the world. Nothing or no one could bring her down. Finally, everything was falling into place. Not only was she finally about to bring home her baby, she and Micah were in a good place. Not wanting to be separated from her baby during the early years, she'd put in her notice at the detention center. She wanted to give her daughter the best of everything and that included having a full-time parent.

Iman pulled into the hospital's parking lot and then reached into her purse to find her phone. She wanted to call and let Micah know she'd arrived and to meet her on the maternity ward. Upon retrieving her phone, she saw that he'd tried calling her twice and there was a text message from him. *Come to my office when you get here.*

They'd already decided to meet on the maternity ward. His office was on a different floor. Why would he want her to come there? Maybe he was busy with a patient and wanted her to wait, so they could get her together.

Without giving it anymore thought, Iman grabbed her keys and purse and walked inside. She smiled and waved at everyone she met, not caring if she knew them or not. As she approached the elevator, she heard arguing. She turned and recognized the two individuals as the same couple she'd seen the day Alyssa was born. She couldn't make out what they were saying, but they were definitely upset about something.

Still looking back at the couple, Iman stepped onto the elevator.

"Glad I caught you." Micah stuck his hand out to stop the doors from closing.

"Oh my goodness, you scared me." Iman placed her hand over her chest. "I didn't see you there."

He grabbed her by the forearm and led her off. "We need to talk."

"That's them," a woman said. "That's the couple trying to take our grandbaby."

Iman's head snapped in the woman's direction. It was the same woman she'd seen talking loudly moments ago. The lady slung her long, matted up synthetic hair over her shoulder and pointed her finger towards Iman. Her nails were painted gold and they were so long, they'd started to curve.

Iman looked at Micah. "What's that lady talking about?"

"That's why I called you. They must be Destiny's parents. Dr. Rudolph called and told me—"

Iman shook her head. "Please tell me this isn't happening."

The couple started to approach Iman and Micah. Two guards appeared along with Dr. Rudolph. "We received a call about a disturbance. What seems to be the problem?"

"Yeah, there's a problem. This—"

One guard put his hand up to stop the woman from speaking. "I'm addressing Dr. Rudolph."

Dr. Rudolph turned to Destiny's parents. "If you continue to behave in this manner, I will be forced to have the both of you escorted out."

"Not without my grandbaby you won't," the lady said.

"We've already signed the paperwork." Iman's eyes watered. "Destiny wanted us to have her."

"Let's all take this into my office," Dr. Rudolph said.

With the exception of Iman, everyone started in the direction of Dr. Rudolph's office. Micah stopped when he noticed his wife wasn't next to him and turned to her. She felt Micah's gaze but refused to look in his direction. She felt it deep in her gut. A feeling she'd come to know well. She'd felt it moments before each miscarriage. She'd felt it each time the doctor walked into the exam room to tell her in-vitro didn't work; she'd felt it the day Maya called to tell her the children were moving back in with their mother.

Without saying a word, Iman turned in the opposite direction of Dr. Rudolph, the guards, and Destiny's parents and headed towards the exit.

Micah ran to catch her. He put his hand on her shoulder, but she snatched away and kept walking. "Iman, wait."

She didn't stop. It was over. She was well aware that blood trumped anything else. She had no desire to battle it out in Dr. Rudolph's office, a court of law, or anywhere else. She was exhausted. There was nothing anybody could say that would convince her to stay and fight. "I'm done," she said once she reached the exit.

Micah stopped in front of her. "I think we should at least hear them out. We don't know the whole story. For all we know, they could be crazy, have a criminal record. There was a reason Destiny didn't want them to know."

Iman shook her head. "It doesn't matter. I don't want a fight." She stopped next to her car and rested her back on it. This was the last straw. Iman was done getting her hopes up, only to be disappointed. Children were not in her future.

"You can't give up, baby. We've waited so long. You've waited even longer than me." He continued to look into her eyes, until she turned her head slightly and looked straight ahead. "Do you mind if I go in and get the whole story? David is meeting us here. If anyone can win this for us, he can."

Not only was David was one of the best lawyers Iman had ever seen, he'd become a great friend to them. He rarely lost a case but, at that moment, it didn't matter to Iman. She didn't have the energy to fight another losing battle.

"What's the use?" Iman stared straight ahead, her voice barely above a whisper.

"When the social worker came for the kids, you said I should've done something. I should've tried to reason with her. Anything. Remember that?"

When she didn't respond, he continued. "I owe it to us and possibly that beautiful little girl in there to at least try."

Iman blew out an exasperated breath. "Don't you get it? It's never going to happen. I've accepted it. You should be happy. I mean, you've tried to get me to let this obsession go, right? Now, you have your wish. No more expensive fertility drugs. No more using our savings for in-vitro fertilization. No more sneaking behind your back making appointments with surrogate agencies."

She opened the door and slid into the seat. She turned to her husband, who stood watching her helplessly. "I'm not meant to be a mother." She fastened her seat belt and closed the door.

Chapter *Thirteen*

For the next three days, Iman stayed in bed and refused to discuss anything that concerned children. She'd barely said two words to Micah or anyone else for that matter. She'd ignored phone calls from Maya and her pastor. She'd become so annoyed with calls and text messages she turned her phone off.

Vivian gave a light tap on Iman's bedroom door and pushed it open. "Hey, sweetie. How ya feelin'?"

When Iman didn't respond, she walked inside carrying a tray with a covered bowl and a glass. Iman inhaled the scent of her all-time favorite food before Vivian set it down. She was playing dirty. No matter how Iman felt growing up, her grandmother's chicken and dumplings from scratch always made it better. She wasn't so sure it would work this time.

"I know you said you didn't want anything, but I made you some chicken and dumplings and some iced tea."

Iman rolled over. "Like you used to do it when I was a kid?"

Vivian sat the tray on the nightstand next to Iman. She grabbed the glass and held it out to her. Iman sat up and adjusted her pillows behind her. She reached out and accepted the drink. "Thanks." She took a sip and closed her eyes. It was perfect, just like she remembered it. The taste of it brought back fond childhood memories. She saw herself and all of her cousins in the backyard on the fourth of July eating barbecue, listening to music and doing the electric slide. Being the youngest of the family, her cousins always came over the night before to show her new dances, so she wouldn't be lost. She hadn't seen them in so long. She'd started to feel a longing for the good old days. It wasn't until that very moment that she realized how much her family had meant to her at one time. Dancing in her tiny bedroom, they always had to be in the same formation. Leslie was on the far right, Denise on the far left, Iman stood to the left of Leslie, and Tiana stood.

She opened her eyes and handed the glass back to her grandmother.

"You want anything to eat?" Vivian sat on the side of the bed.

Iman shook her head. "Maybe later."

Vivian continued to look at her. "You ain't ate in days. You can't go on like this."

"What time is Ms. Wanda coming?" Iman asked.

"She's not. I told her I wasn't goin'."

"Don't do that on my account. I'll be fine." Iman removed the pillows that had her head lifted up. She lay back down and pulled the covers over her. "Besides, Micah has taken a few days off. So, if you're worried I'll be here alone and do something to myself, don't. I know how much you were looking forward to going with the church ladies."

Wanda had invited Vivian to go with some of the women from her church to a cabin in the mountains for three days. Iman was shocked that Vivian had considered cancelling her flight to extend her visit. She'd learned from Micah that Vivian had cancelled her flight the night she found out Destiny decided to keep the baby. Turned out, her parents weren't upset with her in the least. They were regular, hardworking people that spent too much time working and not enough time at home. They were strict and Destiny assumed they would put her out. Looks could be deceiving and loud and ghetto didn't mean criminal.

"Let's make a deal," Vivian said. "I'll call Wanda right now, if you take at least five bites from these dumplins'."

Iman didn't need much coercing. She wanted Vivian out of her hair and she knew the dumplings wouldn't disappoint. She cut her eyes at her and sat up straight. "Fine. I'll eat it."

Satisfied that Iman had cleaned her plate, Vivian picked up the tray of food and walked out of the room.

Iman got out of bed and went into her closet. She grabbed her purse and sat on the bed. She sifted through the contents, looking inside every pocket. She'd given Micah her pill bottle, but she hoped one had fallen out. She needed to get her emotions together. She felt out of control and one or two pills would make everything better.

Unsuccessful at finding what she was looking for, she put her things back into her purse and walked into the master bathroom. She opened the medicine cabinet and searched for something, anything to pull her out of the funk she was currently in. She pulled out a medicine bottle and flipped it to the back. It wasn't what she hoped for, but it'd do for now. She opened it, placing two sleeping pills in her hand and swallowed a cup of water behind them.

Chapter Fourteen

"Have you decided what you're wearing to the fundraiser tonight?"

Iman dropped her bags onto the bed and began pulling out and organizing the contents.

"You've been shopping. Again?"

"Yep." Iman walked to the closet and grabbed a few hangers and proceeded to hang the clothes she'd purchased.

Micah trotted to Iman's side of the bed and rummaged through her things. "You spent $1200 at Neiman Marcus." His eyes bucked. "What did you spend over $1500 on at Tiffany's? You barely wear jewelry. This is not like you."

Iman grabbed the receipts from Micah's hand. "First, you're complaining about me laying around all day. Now, you're mad because I've been shopping a few times. Besides, why do you care? I spent this from my personal account. I work or at least I used to work. I should be able to enjoy the fruits of my labor from time to time."

"That's not the point," Micah said. "You're wasting money."

"Like you said." Iman pulled out two pairs of shoes she'd just purchased. "This isn't like me. For years, I've saved and pinched pennies and for what? Children I'll never have." She walked to her full-length mirror and placed the new black cocktail dress in front of her, turning from side to side. "Not anymore. I'm about to start living. I got something for you too."

Micah watched the woman he'd been married to for three years and looked as if he didn't recognize her. "Are you sure you're okay?"

"Never better."

He walked closer to her and grabbed her hand and turned her to face him. "I think you should talk to someone. A professional."

Releasing his hand, she walked to her bed and grabbed a Victoria's Secret bag and pulled out a short, red see-through teddy and held it to her body.

Micah's facial features softened as he stared at her.

Men are so easy, she thought. She reached into another bag and withdrew four-inch red pumps. "You want me to return these?"

"No." He licked his lips. "You can keep those."

Iman smiled. "I thought you'd like them. Why don't you get comfortable while I slip into this and then, who knows?" She sashayed over to him and pulled his body firmly against hers, kissing him with more passion than she'd kissed him in months, causing him to groan. Their hearts beat rapidly. He wanted her right then and there. He returned the kiss with force. She wanted him as badly as he wanted her.

Micah lifted her off the floor and she wrapped her legs around him.

She pulled away to catch her breath. "Wait."

"Why?" He said breathlessly.

"I want to model for you."

"You can model later." He placed her on the bed and proceeded to undress her, pulling her blouse apart. Buttons scattered across the bed. Once her clothes were completely removed, she helped him undress.

Iman looked over at her husband, who was sleeping soundly. Hopefully that performance would keep him off her back for a while. She slid out of bed, put on her workout gear and headed to the gym.

"Where have you been?" Micah asked as soon as Iman walked into the kitchen.

"At the gym. Why?"

"I've left a dozen messages on your cell and I've texted you."

"I left my phone here." She gave him a once over. He was dressed in a black tuxedo. "Why are you all dressed up?"

"Did you forget about the fundraiser I'm speaking at tonight?"

"Ohhhh," Iman sang with little enthusiasm. "Was that tonight? I completely forgot." She drank the rest of her amino acids from her sports bottle. "I don't have anything to wear."

"You mean to tell me you've spent well over $5,000 on clothes and shoes this week alone and you don't have anything to wear?"

"Nothing formal." She placed her water bottle on the counter and turned to him. "No biggie. I'll run upstairs and shower. We can stop and get something on the way. I can change in the dressing room. It won't take long to fix my hair."

Micah looked at his watch. "There's no time. In case you forgot, I'm the keynote speaker. I can't be late.

"Want me to meet you there?"

Micah shook his head. "I'll have one of the nurses to escort me in."

"Would that be nurse Candi?" Iman placed her hands on her hips and glared at Micah.

"What?"

"Don't act like you don't enjoy the attention she gives you. I've seen you two flirting."

Micah laughed. "Woman. You are delusional."

"Admit it. You never wanted me to come. If you did, you would've reminded me. You want to cozy up with the new nurse."

Micah closed his eyes and inhaled. "I don't have time to do this right now." He grabbed his keys from the key holder on the wall. "Good night." He opened the door and left.

After showering and styling her hair, Iman decided she had time to make a drive up the street to a little boutique that sold formal wear. She wasn't in the mood to be social, but she didn't want to give Candi reason to believe her husband was fair game. She paid for the dress and went into the dressing room to change. She'd chosen a black, floor-length halter dress with a side split that stopped just above her knee. Simple, yet chic.

It would take thirty minutes to get there, but she should be there in time to hear Micah speak.

"Good evening, Mrs. Carrington," the gentleman at the door said as soon as she entered the building. "Please, come right in."

Iman entered the ballroom and took a quick scan, hoping to catch Micah before he was seated. According to the program she'd just been handed, the first hour was set aside for the silent auction and networking. She had at least fifteen minutes before Micah took his post.

Without thought, she grabbed a glass of wine from a tray as a waiter walked by. She downed it before he could make his way to the other side of the room and then grabbed another when a different waiter approached. She took notice of the many familiar guests, as they frequented the same functions quite often. The room was filled with important people in the community. Doctors, lawyers, professors and engineers were among the crowd. Then, there were the plus ones. Those who'd begged and possibly paid their friend to bring them, in hopes of finding their perfect mate. Looking around at the women whose dresses didn't leave much to the imagination, she wondered if Candi was present.

After taking a final sip, she placed the glass on a table and grabbed another. She looked around for another employee of the oncology specialty and locked eyes with Erica. Upon mutual recognition, they walked towards each other.

"Hi, Mrs. Carrington. I thought you weren't coming." The women embraced.

"When are you going to stop with this Mrs. Carrington and call me Iman?"

"Sorry. Force of habit."

"Have you seen my husband?" Iman looked around the room once more.

"Yes. I'll take you to him. He's backstage in one of the rooms going over his speech."

"Thanks. Lead the way." Iman followed Erica to the back.

"Here's his room. Would you like me to alert him of your presence?"

Iman shook her head and smiled. "We're not at the office. I think I can handle it from here."

After Erica had gone back into the ballroom, Iman pulled out her compact mirror and did a double take of her hair. She applied a light gloss to her lips. Ruby woo lipstick tended to dry her lips.

Before she reached Micah's dressing room, the door opened. Iman couldn't believe her eyes. Candi was coming out of Micah's private room, adjusting her too short, hot pink dress.

Candi closed the door and leaned against it, inhaling a deep breath. She had the look of a woman thoroughly satisfied. Candi straightened and her eyes connected with Iman. With a wink and a slight smile, she walked in the other direction.

Iman sauntered to the door and placed her hand on the doorknob. Remembering how she'd lost it before when placed in a similar position, she wouldn't risk that happening again. She could stay and act as if she didn't know anything or she could go home and confront him there.

One thing Iman wasn't good at was pretending. If she'd stayed, she'd end up in jail for hurting both Micah and Candi. Instead, she turned and walked down the hall and didn't stop until she reached the exit.

Once the valet brought her car, she sat inside and let the tears take over. She put her key into the ignition and thought it best to call a cab. She'd had three glasses of wine and judging by the way her head was throbbing, it wasn't a good idea for her to drive.

During the cab ride home, Iman thought about all of the bad things that'd happened in her life. She wondered what was wrong with her that she couldn't keep the men in her life happy. She was a beautiful woman. Intelligent. Educated. She wasn't the most fun person to be around lately, but she wasn't a complete bore.

She shouldn't have been too surprised to catch Micah with another woman. No matter how much a man said he loved her, the barren thing would eventually turn out to be too much.

Iman didn't think she could handle another failed marriage. She was sure to end up alone after letting Micah go. She would just stay there, suck it up and deal with it. She could change.

After paying the cab driver, Iman went inside, grabbed the wine bottle she'd put in the back of the fridge before she left and headed upstairs.

"It's almost nine. If you don't get up, we're going to be late for church. You know how hard it is to get a parking spot."

Iman pulled the cover over her head. "Go without me."

"I've gone without you two weeks in a row. I went to a fundraiser without you last night. Now get up and get dressed."

"I'm tired and my head is pounding," she slurred and her breath almost knocked him down.

Micah noticed two empty wine bottles sticking out underneath the bed and picked one up. "Have you been drinking?"

He'd found some in the trash bag the week before when he was taking out the garbage. If she wanted a glass every once in a while, he didn't mind. But, she'd always been so adamant about not drinking any alcohol, no matter how low the percentage. He was already concerned. Now, he was beginning to worry more.

He decided to let her sleep it off and he'd deal with it when he got back. "I'm going to get Amari because I promised her she could go with us to church this morning. She'll be disappointed that she didn't get a chance to see you, but I'll figure out something."

"Mmmhmm." Iman turned over on her stomach and started snoring.

Chapter *Fifteen*

Iman rolled over and looked at the clock. She frowned and then reached over to the nightstand and grabbed her phone. *Monday? Was I asleep an entire day?* She stood, grabbed her head and then sat back down. Once she got her bearings, she stood slowly and went into the bathroom to shower. After getting dressed, she went downstairs into the kitchen and made coffee.

While the coffee brewed, she looked out into the garage to see if Micah had left for work. Relieved to find his car wasn't there, she closed the garage door and sat at the counter with her coffee. After the night Iman had, she didn't want to face him. She knew what she saw, but there was a part of her that wanted to believe there was more to the story. She hadn't been the best person to live with lately, but it wasn't enough to push him to another woman.

Iman grabbed her phone and scrolled down the contact list. She needed to talk to someone. Usually when she needed to vent, she'd call Maya. Given her and Micah's history, she didn't feel comfortable with that. Maya was protective when it came to the Carrington family. She scrolled back up and stopped when she came to Leah's name. She tilted her head to her shoulder and looked up. *Leah's a good listener. She always gives sound advice. But I have been ignoring her calls lately.* After going back and forth, Iman finally dialed Leah.

"Hello," Leah answered dryly.

"Leah?"

"Yes."

"Is everything ok?"

"What do you need?" Leah asked curtly.

Iman hesitated before speaking. "We haven't spoken much in a few weeks. I…um… how are you? You busy?"

"Busy enough," she said, barely loud enough for Iman to hear. "Everything is fine. Did you need something?"

Iman was taken back by Leah's response. She was usually talkative and upbeat. "Are you upset with me?"

Leah huffed. "Now, why would you think that Iman?"

"Am I missing something? You don't sound like yourself. You sound as if you don't want to be bothered."

Leah sighed. "How long have we known each other?"

"About four years."

"Right. And during those four years, I've been there for you, even when you didn't ask. I've covered for you at work, prayed for you after your miscarriages, picked up Kendall, Kaitlyn, and Karlos from school when you couldn't get there. You know everything there is to know about me. And, apparently, I don't know anything about you."

"Is that what this is about? I didn't tell you I was divorced?"

"Yes. That's what it's about." Leah laughed. "You know. All this time, I thought we were friends. But, I guess the joke was on me. I sat back and thought about it. I was the one doing all the giving. And, the sad part is I was too dumb to realize you didn't want my friendship. The only thing you care about is having children. Nothing or nobody else in this world matters to you."

Leah continued before Iman could open her mouth to speak, "You don't have to worry about me being in your business anymore."

"I never meant—"

"I don't need an explanation," Leah cut her off. "I get it. You have your friends and I'm not one of them. Now, I get it."

Iman wanted to say something, anything to make it better. Clearly, Leah wasn't in a place to hear what she had to say. It wasn't as if she knew what to say anyway.

The silence settled between them like distant strangers.

"Ugh," Leah sounded exasperated, "I have to go." With that, Leah ended the call.

After taking a few sips of coffee, Iman pushed her mug to the side and placed her head on the kitchen table. She replayed Leah's words over and over in her head. *Am I selfish?*

It's one thing if one person calls you selfish, but after hearing it more times than once, there has to be some truth to it. Until now, she'd never seen herself as selfish or self-centered, but maybe she was. She had been so caught up in what she wanted, she hadn't paid much attention to anything or anyone else around her.

Iman lifted her head from the table and sat up straight. She went into the closet and grabbed her coat. It was time to pay Micah a visit.

Chapter *Sixteen*

She pulled into the hospital's parking lot. After putting the car in park, Iman massaged her temples. Her head was pounding. She figured it was stress induced. She reached into her purse and took two aspirin. She then laid back and closed her eyes. She wanted to get her thoughts together before approaching Micah.

Erica wasn't at her usual post, so she headed towards Micah's office and stopped when she saw him coming out of an exam room. She started walking towards him, but paused when she saw Nurse Candi trailing close behind him. Iman stood back and watched their interaction. Once again, Candi was acting too familiar. He stood against the wall looking at the clipboard in her hand. Candi laughed at something and conveniently rubbed her hand down his chest.

Iman wondered what could be so funny. He was an oncologist. There's nothing humorous about cancer.

A scowl appeared on Iman's face when her hand lingered on his body and he didn't seem to be in any hurry to remove it. After a few seconds, they turned. Micah placed his hand on her back, and they walked into a room.

Iman remained in place. Her eyes stinging, heart beating out of control, everything within her wanted to grab something, anything, and knock them both senselessly. She walked towards the room where they'd just entered and stopped. Could she handle what was going on on the other side of the door? She considered herself strong, but there was only so much heartache a person could take.

She placed her hand on the doorknob and inhaled. She opened the door and there they were in full view. The perfect guy. The one constant in her life, wrapped up in another woman's arms. She stood watching, listening, as he called out another woman's name.

The ringing of Iman's phone caused her to jump. Startled, she looked around. She was still in the hospital parking lot. She'd dozed off just that quickly. She was relieved to discover she'd been dreaming. She looked back at her phone. The call was from her niece, Amari. She clicked ignore.

Though it was a dream, she still couldn't get the thought out of her mind of Candi coming out of Micah's dressing room the night of the fundraiser and she wasn't in the mood to go inside and risk running into her. She'd rather wait and talk to Micah once he returned home.

Not in the mood to talk to anyone, nor was she ready to sit at home alone, Iman decided to stop at a restaurant near the hospital and grab a bite to eat. She got out of the car and walked inside Chili's bar and grill. She looked around the room and decided she didn't want a table. She opted to sit at the bar and order something light. She perused the menu for a moment.

"No, Mommy." Iman turned her attention to a little girl who'd fallen onto the floor, squirming and fighting to get her way. Her eyes traveled upward and stopped on the woman's stomach. She looked exhausted and due any day now. No matter how a child behaved - temper tantrums, attitude, anything - she didn't care. She'd take it over no children any day.

"Come here, pumpkin. Daddy's here."

Iman's ears perked upon hearing the familiar male voice. She squeezed her eyes shut and sucked in a mouth full of air. She turned her head slightly to the right and locked gazes with the first man who'd ever broken her heart. It seemed like an eternity had passed before she was able to pull her gaze away and she'd only done so because Cedric, his pregnant wife, and little girl had walked out of the restaurant.

I left him in Georgia. Why is he here? Is he visiting? Is her family from here? Why do I care?

Iman pulled her phone from her purse and Google searched Cedric Slater and read the latest news.

Retired football player is the new sportscaster for WBUP in Baltimore, MD.

She closed her eyes tight and shook her head. *Why? What do I have to do to erase that part of my life?*

She lost her appetite.

She called the bartender over and ordered a Martini. She took a big gulp, draining the drink and ordered another. Before she knew it, she'd lost count. When she attempted to order another, the bartender told her it was against policy to serve her anymore since she was alone and recommended she call someone to pick her up.

"I'm f-f-ine," she slurred. "I know when I've had enough." She swirled around in her chair and attempted to stand. "Whoa." Iman grabbed her head and sat back down. She placed her head onto the bar. She reached into her purse and pulled out her phone. She handed it to the bartender. "Maya," she said. "She'll come for me."

Maya's eyes found Iman as soon as she entered the restaurant. Her eyes widened and her mouth dropped. With hurried steps, she headed towards the bar where Iman was seated.

"Iman." Maya lifted her head off the bar and examined Iman's face.

"Heeeeey girl. I knew you would come. I love you so much."

Maya glanced around the restaurant and then turned back to Iman. "What are you thinking coming out here in broad daylight getting drunk?"

"I have no friends, they took my baby, and Micah don't love me no more." Iman's eyes glazed over and her head lolled from side to side. "Why does God hate me?" Her body slumped as she finally rested her head on Maya.

"What are you talking about? God doesn't hate you. Micah loves you and I'm your friend."

"You're Micah's friend."

"We need to get you home."

"No. I can't go back there."

"Can you help me get her to my car?" Maya asked the bartender.

Chapter *Seventeen*

Iman closed her eyes as soon as she'd tried to open them. Her head was pounding. She squinted and glanced around the room. She sat up slowly with her head in her hands and blinked until her eyes adjusted to the lights. She recognized Maya's living room.

"What am I doing here?"

"Mmm-mmm-mmmm." Maya walked in and sat in a chair across from her. She handed her a cup of coffee and a few saltines. "You don't remember leaving Chili's with me?"

Iman's eyebrows dipped as she forced her mind to remember. She released a long sigh. "I guess I had too much to drink."

"Maybe a little," Maya said. "Are you ready to talk?"

Iman shook her head.

"Micah's called a few times. He's worried about you."

Iman stood. "He doesn't need to. I'm fine." She looked around the sofa where she'd slept. "Where's my purse?"

"I put it up. I'll get it for you after we talk."

"What time is it? How long have I been here?"

Maya looked at her phone. "It's a little after six."

Iman's eyes bucked. "After six? I've been here for six hours?"

Maya nodded.

"Look. I don't have time for a heart to heart. I appreciate you coming to get me, but all I needed was a ride. Now, please. Are you going to take me to get my car or do I need to call a cab?"

Maya stared at Iman, clearly irritated. "Fine." She stood. "I'll get your keys, but tell me something."

"What is it, Maya?" Iman snapped.

"Do you really believe I'm Micah's friend and not yours?"

"What?"

"When I picked you up earlier, you said you have no friends."

"I was drunk, Maya. Why are you letting something like that get to you? I don't even recall saying it."

"Whatever." Maya turned and walked into the kitchen and grabbed Iman's purse and brought it to her. "Here's your purse." Not waiting for Iman to respond, Maya walked outside.

Chapter Eighteen

Iman's forehead crinkled when she pulled up to her home and saw Maya and their pastor's car parked in front.

She pulled into the driveway and pushed the button on the remote that opened the garage. She got out of her car, popped open the trunk, and pulled out as many bags as she could carry in one trip. She would come back for the rest later.

Micah met her at the kitchen door that led to the garage and grabbed the bags from her hands. "There's a few more in the car."

He set the bags on the counter and skimmed through them. "What's all this?" He began pulling out the items. Everyone sat and watched in silence.

Iman looked from Micah to Maya, who was sitting on a bar stool rummaging through Iman's bags, looking just as confused as Micah. She then turned her attention to her pastor, Dr. Christensen, who was seated at the dining table next to her grandmother. "Hi, Dr. C." She walked up and gave her a big hug. "What are you guys doing here?"

"Oh, nothing much. Just wanted to see how you were doing."

Iman smiled. "I'm great. I decided to do a little Christmas shopping." She kissed Vivian on the cheek. "Did you enjoy your trip?"

"It was fine," Vivian said.

"You did a lot of Christmas shopping," Micah said.

"It's two weeks before Christmas and you can't even tell just by looking around here."

"It doesn't look like Christmas because you took everything down." Micah said. "Remember?"

She turned and went to Maya. She grabbed her arm. "Hey, girl. Come help me get the rest of the stuff out the car." She smiled wide. "I'm so glad you're here. I haven't seen you in what, almost a week? Thought you were mad at me. Since you're here, you can help me decorate. She looked around. "You all can help. I'm doing it big. We're going to put up lights outside. I bought a huge Santa and reindeer. I even got a nativity scene out there."

Everyone kept giving each other sideways glances, but Iman pretended not to notice.

"Baby." Micah walked up to her and grabbed her hand. "Are you sure you're okay?"

Iman looked up and kissed Micah on his cheek. "Never better." She smiled. "Wanna help me get this stuff out the car?"

"Let's do that later." He looked to Dr. C. for support.

"Yes, dear." Dr. C. stood. "Let's talk."

Iman's eyes darted from one person to the next. "Okay," She said hesitantly before sitting in between Vivian and Dr. C. Micah and Maya sat in the other chairs.

"What's up?" Iman asked.

"Micah," Dr. C. said, "why don't you tell Iman why we're here."

All eyes were on Micah. "Please don't be upset with me for this, but I'm worried about you."

"Why? I feel great. This is the best I've felt in years."

"You just had your biggest dream taken from you and you didn't shed a tear," Micah said softly. "You won't talk about it. You've accused me of having an affair. You're drinking way too much and—"

"Drinking?" Vivian interrupted.

"It's nothing, Mama. We'll discuss it later." Iman squinted her eyes and pleaded with Vivian not to say anything further.

"The only thing I've seen you do for the last few days is shop," Micah continued. "I've never seen you act so irresponsible with money. If you don't slow down, we're going to go bankrupt. You've even started spending money from your parents' insurance policy."

"Why is that any of your business? It's my money to spend however I want."

"No." Micah looked as if he was struggling to keep his voice steady. "When we went into our savings to perform all of the expensive fertilization treatments, we agreed to not spend any of that money unless it was absolutely necessary."

"You can't be serious." Iman stared at Micah. "You called everyone here to embarrass me? You want to call me out about a few thousand dollars I spent?" Iman stood. "The entire time we've been married, I've spent every waking moment worried about a child that doesn't even exist and now that I'm not, you want to have an intervention? I figured you'd be happy about it."

Micah stood and moved in front of Iman. "Why would I be happy about that?"

"Forget it." Iman grabbed her keys from the counter. "You guys can finish this conversation without me. I'm leaving."

"Iman, wait—"

Dr. C. walked over and touched Micah's arm. "You mind if I try?" Without waiting for a response, she followed Iman out to her car.

"You wanna do it here or go to my office?" Dr. C. said after Iman let her into the car.

Iman turned the key in the ignition and started to back out of the garage. She got to the end of the driveway and stopped and put the car in park.

Dr. C. had been the one person in her life that she felt she could let it all out with. Maya was her friend, but because of her history with

Micah, she felt she had to hold back. After Iman's divorce from Cedric, Dr. C. had helped her move on. She knew more about Iman than anyone else did. "Why? Why do we need to talk? There's nothing to say. I had a child. Seconds later, I lost her. It's nothing new."

"You don't have to fake it for me, Iman. It's me. I know what having children means to you and I'm not buying this act. None of us are."

"I've boycotted Christmas for years, but it doesn't erase all the crap that has happened to me. I decided I might as well get on board with it." She shrugged. "What's the harm in that?"

"Who are you trying to convince?" Dr. C. asked. "I'm happy you want to celebrate Christmas. It's a wonderful time of year. That's not what has Micah, Maya, Ms. Vivian and I worried. You'd come closer than ever to having your first child and without warning, it was taken from you. You didn't cry. You didn't talk about it. What did you do? You returned every item and then turned into June Cleaver. Cooking, cleaning, and shopping. None of that is you."

Iman looked at Dr. C. out the corner of her eye. "I cook and clean."

"Ha," Dr. C. laughed. "Girl, who are you trying to kid?"

"Well, I clean."

"Micah tells me you haven't been sleeping and when you do fall asleep, you wake up sweating. What are you running away from? You're using all of these things to escape your thoughts. Tell me about them."

"I feel like God is mocking me," Iman said under her breath.

"How so?" Dr. C. asked.

This was why Iman loved her. She could say anything and never get a rise from her. No judgment.

"I keep having these dreams." She inhaled deeply and closed her eyes. "I receive a call from the adoption agency, as I did a few weeks ago. The exact conversation. They offered us a little girl. The dream changes and Micah and I are constantly arguing about my not respecting and trusting him. During the next scene there's a nursery in my home with a baby girl, twin boys running around and a teen, but I can never see her face."

Dr. C. remained quiet, so Iman continued.

"I just want this to be over. I'm tired of getting my hopes up for nothing. I don't want to think about it." Tears clouded her eyes. "It hurts too bad. This time was worse than the miscarriages and failed attempts. I held her in my arms. I rocked her. I gave her a name. It was the best few weeks of my life and then she was taken from me. It hurt worse than the foster children being taken. I always knew in the back of my mind they would eventually leave. It was hard watching it happen, but I was more prepared for that." Iman shook her head. "I can't take another heartbreak. I won't go through that again."

She closed her eyes and leaned her seat back. "I don't sleep because it feels like God is dangling children in my face or maybe it's the devil. I don't know. Not only that, I keep dreaming about my cousin."

"The one who—"

"Yeah," Iman interrupted. "Her."

"What's the dream?"

"She's trapped in a small room. Her hands and feet are tied. She's fighting to release herself but can only free one hand. With that one hand, she's reaching out to me and pleading to be released. I'm constantly going back and forth, trying to decide if I want to help her. Once I make a decision and reach for her, the dream about the children begins. I feel like I'm losing it."

Dr. C. stared ahead and looked thoughtful. She then looked at Iman. "Have you tried reaching out to her?"

Iman remained silent. "We spoke."

"And?"

"She's been stalking me. I told her I didn't want to hear anything her trifling, home wrecking behind had to say… give or take a few words." Dr. C. cocked her head to the side and stared at Iman.

"Don't look at me like that. I am not trying to get caught up in her drama. She's probably trying to scheme, as usual."

Dr. C. pursed her lips and shook her head. "Not a good pattern, Iman."

"What?"

"You can't ignore your problems. You'll lose your sanity. Tell Micah what's in your heart and find out what's going on with Ti—"

Iman held up her hand. "Don't say it."

"Tiana. Tiana. Tiana," Dr. C. said. "Not saying her name will not make what happened go away. Nothing will. Deal with it. You don't have to do it alone. Take Micah with you."

"I'm not bringing my husband anywhere near her."

"I'll go with you if you like. I'm sure Maya or Ms. Vivian feels the same. You are not alone in this world, Iman. You have a lot of love here. Why can't you see that?"

"I do."

"No. Really?" Dr. C. pointed towards the front door. "Do you see that?"

Maya and Micah stood at the door watching and Vivian was looking through the window.

They laughed.

Iman released a long sigh and laid her head back on the headrest.

"You might as well let it all out." Dr. C. said after Iman's mood changed.

"Micah's having an affair."

Dr. C. didn't respond.

Iman lifted her head and turned it towards Dr. C. "Did you hear what I said? Micah's having an affair."

"I heard you." Dr. C. said calmly. "Are you sure?"

Iman nodded. "I saw them."

"In the act?"

"I saw her coming out of his dressing room."

"And?"

"And." Iman continued. "Her clothes were messed up and it was obvious what she'd been doing."

"What did Micah say when you confronted him?"

Iman shrugged and turned her head away.

"Just as I thought," Dr. C. said. "Never assume anything. Talk to your husband, okay?"

"I will."

"Now, go inside and love on the family God has given you. I'm going to go home and be with mine."

Iman nodded her head. "Yes, ma'am. And thank you."

Dr. C. patted her shoulder. "Let me know how it goes with your cousin. And, before I forget," Dr. C. said, "Dreams aren't always cut and dry. I don't know the details of what yours mean, but I will pray on it. When you mentioned an older girl in your dream, I saw your niece's face. I've only seen her a few times, but each time, I felt a strong connection between you two. I know she desires a closer relationship with you. She needs you."

Iman recalled the times Amari had called her and she'd ignored or didn't return her calls. She also thought about the last few weeks that Amari had gone to church with Micah. Each time, she'd asked about Iman. She made a mental note to call Amari later that night.

Chapter Nineteen

"Somebody's calling you from Eureka County Jail," Vivian peeked her head inside Iman's bedroom.

"You can hang it up." Iman stepped down off the stepstool where she'd just finished hanging her new John-Richard Slate giclee painting over her bed. She stepped back and looked at her newly decorated bedroom and smiled. She'd maxed out her credit card at Neiman Marcus, but it was worth it. She'd promised herself that would be her last thing. She needed changes and redecorating her room was the change she'd needed.

Noticing Vivian still held the phone in her hand, she decided to take the call. "I'll accept the charges." Iman braced herself for the worse.

"Why are you calling my home?" Iman said as soon as she heard Solei's voice through the receiver. "No, Micah isn't available. Do you have a message for me to give him?" After the few weeks she'd just had, Iman didn't have the strength nor the desire to argue with anyone, especially someone who meant so little to her.

At least this time, the woman didn't have as much attitude. Maybe being locked away humbled her.

"Look," Iman said after Solei asked when was a good time to call back. "I don't know what time he'll be home. Just give me the message and I will—"

Iman's head snapped back like she'd been slapped. "Uh. She hung up on me again." She looked at her grandmother, "Don't answer any more calls from the jail. Okay, Mama?"

Iman followed Vivian into the kitchen, picked up a towel and started wiping off the counter, while Vivian finished washing the few dishes that were in the sink.

"We have a dishwasher."

"I don't trust no machine to clean my dishes like I can. Wanna tell me what the call was about?"

"I don't know. Micah's ex-wife has been calling off and on, but she won't tell me why. She just asks for Micah. I've told him, but he isn't interested in talking to her."

"What's wrong?" Iman looked at Vivian, who was staring at her like she'd lost her mind.

With one hand on her hip, Vivian shook her head. "You okay with your husband talkin' to his ex?"

"She's in jail." Iman shrugged. "What's the worst that can happen?" She peeled a banana and took a bite. "Plus, the sooner he talks to her, the sooner she'll stop calling here."

Iman pulled out her iPhone and scrolled through her emails and checked for missed calls. She shook her head. *No messages or anything?* Iman was out of her mind with boredom. She'd grown tired of sitting home all day alone with her thoughts. Sure, her grandmother was there, but she wasn't much of a talker. She spent the majority of her time with her Bible and a notebook. She'd taken back all the baby items she'd purchased and cancelled all deliveries. When she finished that, she'd cleaned the house from top to bottom and spent the last few weeks shopping. She'd purchased more shoes and handbags in the last few weeks than she had in over five years.

The *Jeopardy* theme song could be heard from the living room. For as long as Iman could remember, her grandmother never missed an episode of *Jeopardy*. If she ever got a chance to be a contestant, Iman believed she'd give them a run for their money. She was that good.

Iman stood in the doorway and watched in silence as Vivian guessed the answers.

"What's on your mind?" Vivian muted the sound when the first commercial started. "You've got about two minutes before the show starts back."

"I appreciate you canceling your flight and staying here with me."

Vivian's eyes squinted and the corners of her lip turned into a small smirk. "Chile, I did that weeks ago. You forgettin' I'm the one that raised you. I know something's on ya mind. Now, what is it?"

Iman let out a soft sigh. "I'm sorry for speaking to you the way I did that day."

Vivian patted the seat next to her, inviting Iman to sit. Iman sat on the opposite end. Vivian shook her head. "I was surprised to hear how you felt and I didn't like your tone, but I'm glad you told me."

Iman frowned. "Why are you smiling? I thought you'd be mad at me."

"You remind me so much of Clara."

Iman had heard that her entire life. Everyone said she looked and acted just like her mother. She'd seen pictures and she agreed there was a resemblance.

"I patted the seat next to me and you're almost a foot away." Vivian chuckled. "Just like her, you're so darn independent. I don't know how to comfort you. I hug people's problems away. You said I'm there for everyone except you. I don't know how to be there for you." Vivian closed her eyes. "When you first came home with me, I tried to rock you to sleep, you screamed and squirmed until I laid you down in your crib. Then, you went right on to sleep."

"Mama. I was three when daddy died. You don't rock a three-year-old."

"I got you long before Ricky died. I got you when you were three months old because he couldn't seem to get himself together."

"But, I remember being with him."

"Yeah. You saw him almost every day. I made sure to take you to see him for a few hours, but I couldn't leave you there. He was too far gone."

"Oh." Iman sat back and listened.

"Remember when those girls across the street jumped you? You couldn't have been older than eight."

"I remember," Iman said softly.

"You came home with your hair all over your head and your clothes ripped up. I grabbed a switch cause' I was goin' to go over there and whoop all of 'em."

Iman laughed. "Yes and I begged you not to."

"Mmmhmmm. And you never shed a tear. Your granddaddy went on over there and talked to their folks anyway, and you didn't talk to us for a week because you said you wasn't some baby that needed taking care of."

"Okay," Iman said. "I get it. I'm not easy to comfort."

"Come on over here." Iman scooted over until her side touched Vivian's. Vivian wrapped her arm around Iman's shoulder and pulled her in close, holding her for a moment.

"This is weird."

"I know and that's my fault. My holding you shouldn't be awkward. I raised you. I should have pushed harder to give you affection. In case I've never said it, I'm proud of you, sugar." Vivian looked around. "You have a wonderful husband this time around. I never did like that Cedric and I think I told ya so."

"Yeah, I should have listened."

"I'd never seen you lose control before that day you went after him with that club."

Iman squeezed her eyes shut. "That definitely wasn't one of my finest moments."

"I don't know," Vivian said. "Though you didn't shed a tear then either, it did show you're human like the rest of us."

"I hate losing control like that."

"Being here with Micah and your pastor has been good for you. How are you really holding up? I remember how bad you were after we lost Joe. I don't want to see that happen to you again."

Iman squeezed her eyes shut to try and erase the memory of her grandfather's death. She didn't handle it well. Vivian was the only person aware of just how bad she'd gotten. "It won't."

"I didn't give Tina your—" Vivian felt Iman stiffen. "Let me say my peace and I'll leave it alone." She sighed and then continued. "If you don't do anything else I ask, do this. Hear her out. I'm not asking you to become her best friend again. But, I think what she has to say is worth your time."

One minute, Iman was listening to the soothing sound of her grandmother's voice. The next minute, she was being awakened by the sound of her cellphone ringing.

She sat up and wiped her mouth. "How long have I been asleep?"

"Over an hour," Vivian said.

"And you stayed with me on you all this time?"

Vivian shrugged. "Making up for all the times you needed to be held and I didn't. Besides, you looked exhausted and I didn't want to wake you." Iman grabbed her phone off the coffee table and smiled when she saw her niece's photo. After all this time, she still hadn't returned any of Amari's calls. But, all that was about to change. She would be there for Amari from now on.

"Hey, Amari. How are— What? Okay. Call an ambulance. I'm on my way."

Chapter *Twenty*

Iman made it just in time to see the stretcher being put into an ambulance. She spotted Amari standing on the porch speaking with one of the paramedics and ran to her. "How are you holding up?"

"I'm fine. Thanks for coming." Iman studied Amari's face. She didn't appear shaken or even sad. "Let me go inside and grab my bag. I called Uncle Micah. He's going to meet them in the ER."

Iman scratched her head and then walked inside behind Amari. She hadn't been to their home in months. In fact, the last time she was there was when she, Maya, and Micah were taking turns staying with Hannah each week while she battled leukemia. Everyone thought she was better. But now, looking around the living room, there was an oxygen tank, blankets on the couch, and a small refrigerator in the corner for her convenience. It was setup exactly as it was when she'd been sick before.

"Amari," Iman said when she came back down with her bags. "Has your mom been sick again?"

Amari walked through each room, turning off lights and unplugging everything. "Yes," she said curtly.

"Did Micah know?"

Amari shrugged.

"Why didn't you let us know?"

Amari stared at Iman for a moment and then turned away. "The ambulance is leaving. Can we go now?"

Iman followed Amari outside and reached to help her with her bags.

Amari snatched away from her. "I got it." They rode to the hospital in silence.

"I'm sorry I haven't returned any of your calls."

Amari stared out the window without responding.

"Have you been taking care of things alone?"

"I really don't feel like talking right now."

Iman felt terrible. She'd been so caught up in starting a family of her own, she'd neglected the family she already had. She'd give Amari some time, but she would not give up until she fixed their relationship.

Chapter Twenty-One

Amari ran into Micah's arms when she saw him. He'd just finished speaking with Hannah's doctor.

"How is she?" Iman asked after he let Amari go.

He looked into Amari's big brown eyes. He blinked rapidly to keep tears from falling and released a sigh. Iman touched his arm and pulled him off to the side. "She's on a ventilator," he said. "And she gave specific instructions that she didn't want to be kept alive that way and that she didn't want to burden me with making that kind of decision."

"I don't get it," Iman said. "She had a bone marrow procedure done. I thought she was cured."

"Apparently, the transplant didn't work the way we thought. I'm so angry with her doctor. I've got a mind to sue their pants off."

"It's okay," Amari said. They hadn't seen her walk over. "You don't have to whisper around me. She's going to die, isn't she?"

Micah and Iman struggled with what to say.

"Mom and I have talked about it already. We both knew this day would come. She doesn't want to live on a machine. She's tired of hurting and she just wants to be with Jesus."

Iman swallowed the lump in her throat. She had to keep it together. Amari didn't break, so she couldn't either.

"How long has she been sick?" Micah asked.

"Four months."

"And nobody thought to tell me?" Micah spoke louder than he'd intended.

"I'm sorry. I wanted to tell you both. I tried a few times, actually." She glared at Iman. "But, your wife wouldn't take my call." She turned back to Micah. "She didn't want anyone to know. She has a nurse that comes in for a few hours a day and someone else who comes in and helps with cooking and cleaning. And I help out as much as she lets me."

Micah's gaze landed on Iman's and she lowered her head.

"Why didn't she want anyone to know?"

She motioned her head towards Iman. "She didn't want to run her off like Aunt Solei."

Iman reached out to Amari, this time ignoring her when she resisted. "I've been selfish and into my own world lately. I'm sorry. That changes today. I'm not Solei, baby. I love you and your mom. I would never leave you. I enjoyed spending time taking care of you guys."

Amari pulled away and stepped back. "Whatever. I'm over it. Can I please go in and see my mom now?"

Iman covered her mouth with her hand. She hadn't realized how much she'd hurt Amari. And knowing just how much responsibility had been put on the young teen was killing her inside. She was always so upbeat and acted as if nothing bothered her, kind of like Vivian said Iman was. She'd allowed her own selfish needs to get in the way of what should have been first priority. Her family. Here she was obsessing over starting a family and she already had one who loved and needed her.

Iman would make it right, but now wasn't the time to push. Micah wrapped his arm around Amari and led her into her mother's room with Iman following them.

Chapter *Twenty-Two*

Iman stood next to the kitchen counter and downed a glass of wine. She sat the glass on the counter, stepped back, and leaned against the wall with her eyes shut.

"How many did that make?"

Iman jumped. "What are you doing home this early?"

"I came to see how Amari was doing. We did just bury her mother a few days ago. How is she?"

"Fine, I guess. She's up in her room."

"Have you talked to her?"

Iman rolled her eyes and walked into the living room with Micah on her trail.

"I know this is hard," Micah said. "But, she needs you. You have to figure out a way to get her to open up to you."

"Don't you think I've tried? Anytime she sees me, she rolls her eyes and goes the other way. She just keeps herself locked up in her room all day. That is, until you get here."

"Well, you need to try harder."

Iman cut her eyes towards her husband and frowned. "She's your niece. What are you doing to help? I haven't seen you put forth any effort and I thought you'd taken leave."

Micah sat on the arm of the couch, looking thoughtful. "Maybe you're right." He stood and walked to the bottom of the stairs. "Amari!"

He turned to Iman. "Take her to get the rest of her things from home and then maybe you guys should do some shopping. Go out to eat. Whatever you women like to do."

"Hey, Uncle Micah," Amari said as soon as she came downstairs. She threw her arms around him. "Are you off?"

"No, pumpkin. I just wanted to check on my favorite girls." Amari's eyes connected with Iman's and then she rolled them.

"You're not staying?"

He shook his head. "No. I'm heading back. But, your auntie is going to take you to get the rest of your things."

Amari didn't respond. "Come on," he said. "Walk me to my car while Iman gets ready."

Iman watched Amari mope around her old room. She skimmed over her clothes and shoes but wasn't putting much into her bag. She huffed a few times and slumped her shoulders.

"You okay?" Iman asked.

She shrugged. "I guess."

Iman wasn't sure what Micah had said to Amari, but whatever it was worked. While she wasn't overjoyed to be with her, she was no longer rolling her eyes and ignoring her.

Iman moved from the doorway of Amari's bedroom and stood beside her. After a quick scan of the contents of her closet, Iman frowned. "Are these all your clothes?"

"Yeah," she said breathlessly.

There wasn't much there but, from what Iman could tell, everything looked worn and outdated. "You wanna leave this stuff here and go shopping?"

Amari's eyes lit up. "Can we?"

"Anything you want."

"Good because I really don't want any of my old clothes. They're old and everyone laughs at me. Can we get rid of this stuff?"

"I didn't know you were having problems with kids at school."

Amari looked away. "I know. I wanted to tell you but, when you never answered my calls, I figured you didn't care. Mom never felt like taking me anywhere. Plus, she didn't really have any money since she had to stop working."

Iman closed her eyes and took a deep breath.

"Uncle Micah said I didn't have to hold back with you and that I could say what's been on my mind and you won't get mad." She looked up at Iman. "Is that true?"

Iman nodded.

"What did I do to make you stop loving me?"

Iman wasn't expecting that. She pulled Amari into her arms. "I never stopped loving you."

"If that's true, then why did you stop coming over?" she cried. "I mean. I know you were busy with Kendall, Karlos, and Kaitlyn. But after they left, I just knew I'd be your girl again. We used to do everything together before they came. Why do you love them more?"

Iman lifted Amari's chin with her finger. "Sweetie, I'm so sorry I made you feel neglected. Of course I still love you." Iman wiped the tears that had trickled down Amari's face.

"So, when you get your new baby, will I still get to stay there?"

"There's no baby, sweetie."

Amari squinted. "Yes there is. I saw her."

Amari wasn't with her and Micah when they went to see the baby, so what was she talking about? She didn't take pictures and she didn't recall Micah taking any either. But, she was caught up that day, so maybe he did.

"Did your uncle show you a picture or something?"

Amari shook her head. "I saw her in a dream."

"Is that all? Believe me. Dreams don't always mean what you think." She put her arm around Amari's shoulder and they headed towards the door. "Let's get some shopping done."

Chapter *Twenty-Three*

"Iman!"

Iman bolted from her bed and looked around.

"Iman!"

She stood and headed downstairs. "What is it, Mama?"

"You tell me," Vivian said, glaring at Iman like she was a little girl about to get a spanking.

Iman's eyes followed Vivian's and she dropped her head. Lined across the counter were wine bottles. "It's nothing but some wine bottles, Mama. It's not a big deal."

"It is a big deal, Iman. You do not need to be drinking this stuff again. Do I need to remind you what happened when your granddaddy died? Do you remember how messed up you were?"

"I don't need a reminder. I was there," she snapped.

"Let that be your last time sassin' me. You may be grown, but you will not disrespect me and I don't care if it is your house." She waited. Iman didn't respond, so she continued. "You hit rock bottom behind a bottle and had to live with me for a year and start over. You were single then, but now you have too much at stake. I will not sit back and watch you ruin your life."

Iman leaned her head against the wall and fell silent.

Vivian walked up to her and pulled her eyes open. "Are you drunk now? What's wrong with you, girl?"

"No," she slurred. "I'm not drunk. I just took some sleeping pills."

"Lord ha' mercy. How many?"

"Just two."

"Gone upstairs and sleep them off. But tonight, we're finding you an AA meeting."

"AA Meeting?"

Vivian and Iman jumped.

"Who needs AA?" Micah closed the door and sat his keys down.

Iman and Vivian looked at each other but didn't speak.

Micah kissed Vivian on the cheek and gave Iman a peck on her lips. "You need AA, baby?" He laughed. When he noticed Vivian and Iman weren't smiling, his face became serious. "What's going on?" He looked at Iman. "Is there something I don't know?"

Vivian took off her apron and walked out of the room. "Tell him." She mouthed to Iman before leaving.

"It's no big deal." Iman laughed, but Micah continued to stare at her intensely.

"Do you have an alcohol problem?"

Iman sat down on the stairs. “Can we do this later? I’m tired.”

“No. We’re doing this now.”

Iman took a deep breath. “The months following Granddaddy’s death, I started drinking. A lot. It got so bad I ended up losing my job and my home. I went rehab a few months and moved in with Mama. I went to AA meetings for a few years after that.”

Micah remained silent. He stared at nothing in particular.

“Are you going to say something?”

He stood and walked to the door. “I can’t deal with this right now.”

“You’re leaving? You don’t have anything to say?”

“What do you want me to say, Iman? We’ve known each other four years, married for three. You never thought to tell me this? There’s a lot about you I still don’t know. You constantly go behind my back and do things. Now, you’re keeping secrets. I need to clear my head.”

“Please. Don’t go. Not like this. I’ll answer any questions you have.”

Without responding, he turned and walked outside.

“Iman.” Micah pushed his wife’s shoulder. “Iman. Wake up. You okay?” He wiped the sweat from her forehead with his hand.

Iman had awakened on many occasions in a cold sweat, but this time she had tears in her eyes.

She felt Micah's arms envelop her as he'd done many times before, but this time the images were still at the forefront of her mind.

"You wanna talk about it?"

Iman looked into her husband's eyes and shook her head.

"Is it the same dream?"

She nodded.

After the talk Iman had with Dr. C., she told Micah about the dream. They'd gone away for two nights and then came back worse. This time, Tiana fell through the hole, and her blood flew up and splattered all over her. She looked behind her and saw a baby trapped inside of a wall, screaming to be released.

"You know what you need to do."

Iman nodded again. "I'll talk to Tiana if you talk to Solei."

Micah grunted. "No deal."

"I've got enough to deal with without her calling here every day. What is it going to hurt? "Talk to her next time she calls."

"Okay," Micah sighed. "You call Tiana right now and schedule a meeting with her and I will make myself available if she calls again."

"Micah?"

"What is it?"

"Thanks for sticking by me. I know I'm hard to deal with. I thought you were going to leave me tonight."

He looked into her eyes. "You should know me better than that by now."

They continued to lie in bed in silence. "We still need to talk about your drinking and pill taking."

Iman released a soft sigh. "I threw out the pills last night. Mama already poured out the wine."

"That's a good start, but it's not that easy. If I am to trust you to take care of my niece, I have to know you're taking steps to get better. Not only that, you need to do weekly counseling sessions. I love you with my whole heart, but Amari has been through enough and I won't subject her to life with a drug addict or an alcoholic. You need to learn to deal with disappointment in a healthy manner."

"You hear what I'm saying?" he asked after Iman never responded.

She nodded.

"Let's get through the holidays, but before I go back to work, I need to see a schedule. Mama Vi told me she can stay as long as we need her to."

"Okay."

"Okay?" he said with raised eyebrows. "That's it? No argument?"

She shook her head. "You're right. I need help." She stood and headed to the master bathroom. "Before I forget, remember the lady I told you about? Ms. Bessie?"

"The one from the supermarket with the bad living conditions?"

"Yes, her. I want to do something for her."

"What do you have in mind?"

"I want to have her house fixed up."

"I see no problem with that." Micah sat up and turned his body to the side of the bed and put his feet in his slippers. "Write out a budget and I'll make some calls."

"Already done."

Micah gave Iman a knowing look.

"I didn't schedule anything yet. I just got price quotes." She walked over to her nightstand and pulled out a small writing pad and handed to him. "Look it over and let me know what you think."

After spending the morning volunteering at Damascus, Maya went with Iman to several stores returning the expensive clothing and decor Iman had purchased. She realized not only did she not need the items; she didn't even like any of it.

She'd planned to use the money to take Amari shopping so she could decorate her room however she wanted. They're day of shopping was a success. They'd spent at least five hours at the mall buying clothes, shoes, lotion and perfume spray from Bath and Body Works. They went to the electronics store and purchased a laptop.

It was four days before Christmas and one day before Iman's birthday. For the first time, Iman wasn't dreading either. Though she still didn't intend to have a big birthday celebration, she did agree to let Micah take her out to dinner and spend a night in a luxurious hotel. She'd enjoyed spending her time with Amari. She'd never met a teenager, other than herself, that was so responsible.

Iman dropped Maya off at Dave & Buster's, where their moms had agreed to spend the day with Amari and Tyler. Iman laughed when she looked up and saw Micah coming out to greet her. Apparently, there was more action than they anticipated and they'd called Micah to come and trade places.

Iman sent Tiana a brief text telling her to meet her at a small diner a few blocks away. She'd give her fifteen minutes at most and then she was coming back to spend the day with her family and friends shopping for Christmas.

Iman drove up to the coffee shop fifteen minutes later than she'd agreed upon. She sat in the parking lot and watched Tiana walk inside. It'd only been a few days since she last saw her, and she wasn't sure if it was because she was infuriated at the time or she just wasn't paying attention, but Tiana looked much thinner and the confidence she always had was gone.

She was not in the mood to hear an apology, an explanation, or anything else Tiana was offering because she was over it. She'd moved on and she wished everyone else would too. When she thought about it, losing Tiana didn't mean much because she'd lost her to her ego twenty years ago.

After sitting in the car scrolling through Pinterest, , she decided she'd kept Tiana waiting long enough. She knew it was petty, but that was her right.

Iman stepped inside the diner and looked around until she spotted Tiana. As if on cue, Tiana looked up and waved to her, offering a smile. A smile that looked much too eager for Iman's taste. Iman didn't bother returning the smile. She walked over and sat in the chair across from her, ignoring her attempt to hug her.

Tiana cleared her throat and sat in her chair. "Want me to call the waitress over?"

"No," Iman retorted. "I don't plan to be here long."

Tiana shifted uncomfortably and then took a sip of water. "I appreciate you meeting me today. I know you're busy with your husband and—"

"Like you were busy with my first husband," Iman interjected.

Tiana slumped down in her chair and lowered her head.

Was that shame she saw on Tiana? Remorse maybe? Something had definitely shifted. Tiana wasn't sorry for anything she'd ever done in her life. Even if she was, she was great at hiding it. Iman wasn't sorry for being rude. Tiana deserved it.

After a moment of awkward silence, Iman spoke, "This doesn't have to be ugly. Just tell me what was so important that you needed to say to me so I can leave."

Tiana closed her eyes and took in a deep breath. She placed both hands in her lap and looked up at Iman. "It probably doesn't mean much to you now. But, I'm sorry for the way things went down."

Iman raised an eyebrow. "Things went down? Is that the best you can come up with? In seven years, that's your apology?" Iman was not interested in an apology. But, she refused to let her off that easy.

Tiana glanced around the coffee shop and then back at Iman. "I'm sorry for sleeping with your husband. I'm sorry for calling you and throwing it in your face. I'm sorry for how I treated you in high school and every day since." Tiana grabbed a handful of napkins off the table. She sucked in a breath to try and control her sobs. "I was stupid then and, apparently, I'm still the stupid one."

Trying to keep her composure, Iman still didn't trust her. She refused to let her guard down. "Why now, Tiana? We haven't been cordial in twenty years. Why is it so important for you to make amends now? I gave up years ago. And I still don't know what I did to make you change like that?" Iman wondered why she even cared. She'd buried those feelings years ago. But, something inside of her had to know what caused her cousin, her best friend since birth, the only sister she'd ever known, to just disown her.

"I was jealous, I guess."

"Jealous? Of me?" Iman frowned. "We were all in the same situation. We lived in the same neighborhood, born into the same family and wore the same homely clothes."

Tiana shook her head and shrugged. "You were always better than me, Iman." She fought back tears. "I was always the dumb one. You always made better grades than me. You were prettier," she paused. "Still are. All the boys liked you, even the older guys. It was fine when you weren't at my school. But when you walked in that first day of your freshmen year, my senior year, all the guys were fawning over you, including the one I'd had a crush on for two years. And even after all you've been through, you still came out on top."

"Wait," Iman said. "Who did you have a crush on?"

"Cedric Slater," Tiana said under her breath.

Iman's eyes grew wide. She shook her head. "I had no way of knowing that. Cedric and I didn't start dating until my junior year. You'd gone off to college."

"But, he liked you long before that. You just had your head so caught up in a book, you didn't notice. But, I did."

"Looks like you were mad at the wrong person."

"I know. I said I was the stupid one, didn't I?"

"Whatever," Iman said. "That's the past. It's long gone." Tiana looked as if she wanted to say something. "Anything else? I need to get back."

Tiana took several quick breaths before taking a sip of water.

Iman looked on with caution but didn't say anything. Tiana waved her hand as to say I'll be fine. She took a deep breath. "I have HIV."

Iman waved her hand to signal the waiter.

"Can I get you—?"

"Yeah, an apple martini," Iman said, not giving the waiter time to finish his question.

"You sure you want to do that?"

Iman glared at Tiana. Why would she be asking her if she should have a drink? What does she know and how does she know it? She hated to admit it, but she was thankful for the reminder.

"Make that a coke." Iman said before the waiter turned to leave.

Tiana must have noticed the questions running through Iman's head. "It's ok. I've known for about fourteen months now and I'm confident I can manage."

"I'm sorry to hear that," Iman said sincerely.

"I didn't ask you here for your sympathy. I asked you here because I need a favor."

Iman threw her hands up. "Why doesn't that surprise me?" She stood and grabbed her purse. "You're never sorry about anything."

Tiana stood and touched Iman's arm. "Mimi, please." Tiana didn't attempt to fight the tears that began flowing down her face.

Iman was fed up. Tiana was a master manipulator and Iman wasn't falling for it. She was likely lying about having HIV. But, why? Iman didn't know and she didn't care.

For all Iman knew, Tiana wanted sympathy, so she could somehow get into Iman's house to get close to Micah. She refused to get sucked into her drama. Not this time. Iman ignored her tears and sped out of the diner. Refusing to look back in fear that she'd feel an ounce of sympathy, she didn't stop until she was inside her car.

Chapter Twenty-Four

"Oh. My. Gosh." Amari smiled wide. "It's perfect. My room is so cute," she squealed.

"Before I forget." Iman handed her a gift-wrapped box. "This is for you."

Amari's head leaned slightly to the right and her forehead crinkled. "In case you forgot, Auntie. It's your birthday, not mine."

"Just open it."

"Not until you open yours."

Iman's eyebrows went up. "You bought me something?"

"Well, no. I wanted to, but I didn't have enough money to get something nice. I made it." She flopped down on the bed. "It's probably stupid. Now, I don't want to give it to you."

"Girl, you better give me my present." Iman didn't care if the gift was a spray painted seashell. For the first time in her life, she was excited to receive a birthday gift.

Amari stood and walked to her closet. She reached into the back and pulled it out.

"Wow," Iman said. "It's huge. How did you hide this from me?"

"It wasn't easy. Trust me. You're always somewhere lurking."

"Give it to me." Iman fidgeted like a schoolgirl and grabbed the item from Amari's hand and sat on her bed. She carefully tore the wrapping paper from it. Immediately, tears rolled from her eyes.

"Did you paint this yourself?"

Amari nodded.

Iman kept her eyes glued to the painting.

"Can you tell what it is?"

"My dream." Iman's mouth hung open. "How did you know?" The painting was of two adults holding hands. A baby girl, two small boys and an older girl were next to the adults.

"I've been working on this for over a year. I keep having this dream about all of us here in this house. So, I just drew what I saw. Once I was saw the entire picture, I painted it. I finished it two months ago."

Iman couldn't take her eyes off the painting.

"You don't like it, do you?"

Iman reached out and pulled Amari close to her. "Other than your mom entrusting us with you, this is the best gift anyone has ever given me.

"Iman!" Micah yelled from downstairs.

"We're up here."

She walked out and met Micah in the hallway. He looked worried. "What's wrong?" Iman asked.

"Hey, sweetie." He kissed Amari on her forehead.

"Ewww." She wiped it off. "Would you please stop doing that?" She went into her room and closed the door.

"Is it me or has her entire personality changed overnight? She used to love my kisses," Micah said as he walked down the hall.

Iman shrugged. "I think a weight has been lifted. She wasn't able to be a regular teenager because she was so worried about Hannah."

Iman followed Micah into their bedroom. "I hate to do this to you on your birthday."

She stopped in her tracks. *Not again,* she thought. Things were going too well. It was her birthday. Nothing good could come of that. "It's Candi, isn't it? Are you leaving me? Is she pregnant?"

Micah stared at Iman as if she had two heads. "You don't think much of me, do you?" He stopped adjusting his tie and walked around to where she stood. He pulled her into his arms. "Nothing has ever happened between Candi and me. I'm not the least bit attracted to her. Okay?"

She nodded.

"Anyway. I had her transferred to the maternity ward."

"Really? When?"

"Days after the fundraising event. After hearing how strongly you felt about her, I decided it wasn't worth it."

"Oh." Iman released the breath she'd been holding. She still hadn't told him she'd showed up that night. She was afraid he'd admit to having feelings for her and leave. Leaving would mean he'd take Amari with him and she didn't think she could handle that well. He seemed sincere enough. "Did you and Candi have sex?"

"What? No! Why would you think something like that?"

"I came to your fundraiser. Erica brought me to your dressing room and I saw Candi walk out fixing her clothes."

Micah's forehead wrinkled and he sat on the bed with his head bowed. He looked up to his wife. "You came?"

She nodded.

"When you walked inside the room, what did you see?"

"I couldn't convince myself to go inside."

"Had you stuck around longer you would have noticed that Dr. Lindsey was inside, not me. He and I had to share rooms because some of the others had flooded, so there was a shortage."

"Oh." Iman flopped down on the bed. "Sorry."

"I'm not Cedric. You can trust me."

They sat in silence for a few minutes, until Iman broke the silence. "So, what's your big news?"

"I got a call from my attorney."

"Your attorney? Why?"

"He was contacted by Solei's lawyer. They wanted to serve me at work but—"

"Served? For what?"

"I don't know yet. He called and left a message while I was with a patient. When I returned his call, he said he couldn't go into detail and that he would tell me everything on the way to the airport."

Iman frowned. "Airport? You're leaving?"

Micah sighed. "David thought it would be wise for me to make a trip to Las Vegas tonight. My plan is to get back so we can spend Christmas together. This year may be hard for Amari, you know, not having her mom here."

"Is that trick trying to sue you? Didn't she get enough of your money the first time around?"

"I wouldn't put anything past her," he said. "I'm sorry we have to cancel your birthday dinner. I promise I'll make it up to you."

Iman waved her hands towards him. "Don't worry about that. Amari has already made my day perfect."

"What'd she do?"

Iman looked over Micah's head into the doorway. "Ask her yourself."

Amari smiled and walked into their room. "Sorry for interrupting. I wanted to say thank you for my new phone." Her smile grew wide. "You got me the iPhone 7?"

Micah frowned. "You got her an iPhone?"

"This is the best day ever. I don't need anything for Christmas. I have everything I want."

"I swear, she's the best teenager ever," Iman said.

"Let's see if you're still saying that when she's sixteen."

Amari laughed. "I'll always be amazing, Uncle Micah."

"I'm sure you will. Come here. Let me see your phone."

She walked all the way into the room and handed him the phone. They sat side by side on the edge of the bed and looked at it together.

"Your phone is more hi-tech than mine, girl."

"I love it so much. Aunt Mimi is the best."

"Oh, she's Aunt Mimi now?"

Amari laid her head on his shoulder. He kissed her forehead.

"Come here." Micah patted the seat next to him. After Amari sat, he put his arm around them both. "I'm glad you two are together again. I'm going to get back as soon as I can. What are you going to do while I'm gone?"

Iman looked at Amari. "Probably order some pizzas and watch some movies."

"Can Ms. Maya and Tyler come?"

Micah looked at Iman, who gave a slight smile but didn't say anything. He then turned his attention to Amari. "Why do you want them to come? Is there something I should know?"

Amari looked to Iman for help.

"I'm sure she's asking because she knows Maya and I are friends and Tyler is the only person around her age that we both know." She glanced at Amari. "Right?"

Amari nodded her head quickly. "Yes. And he has cool games on his iPad. I was hoping he could show me how to download some of them on my phone."

Micah's eyes darted from Iman to Amari. "I'm not buying it." He looked at Amari. "You're only fourteen. Wait a few years before you start thinking about boys. Do we need to have the talk before I go?"

Amari stood. "No! Please. We're just friends, I promise." She backed away until she got to the door. "I'm going to pick out a movie."

Micah and Iman looked at each other and laughed. "She got out of here fast," he said.

"Before I forget," Iman pulled out the top drawer of her nightstand and handed Micah a notepad.

"What's this?" He asked.

"My counseling schedule for the next two months. Dr. C. recommended a substance abuse counselor."

Micah pulled Iman into a tight hug. "I'm proud of you baby."

"I want to do something before you go." Iman stood and went to the doorway that led to the hall and called after Amari. "Amari, come here a minute!" She tore three pages from her notepad and handed one to Amari and one to Micah. "Let's do something before you go. Each day, let's write one thing we're grateful for and put it in this jar. It's supposed to help us keep things in perspective."

Everyone jotted something on the paper and placed it in the jar.

"For the first time in a long time, we are in a good place and I want to keep it that way." Iman said. "A lot has happened recently and I think we need to come together and pray more as a family. Starting now."

They all joined hands and Micah led them in prayer.

Chapter *Twenty-Five*

It was the morning of Christmas Eve and Iman looked forward to the next few days. Micah still hadn't come home, but he'd called her this morning to tell her everything was fine and that he had a surprise for her when he returned home that evening. She'd tried as hard as she could, but he wouldn't give her any hints.

It was a little past nine, and she and Amari were on their way to meet with the home improvement company she'd hired to fix up Ms. Bessie's home. She didn't know her very well but, from what she could see, Ms. Bessie was a proud woman so she hoped this wouldn't offend her. She'd wanted to call and let her know she would be stopping by, but she never got her phone number and no one at Damascus seemed to know anything about her. They didn't even know who she was, which was strange since Ms. Bessie had told her she helped out a few days a week.

"Does Tyler have a cell phone?" Amari asked.

Iman briefly took her eyes off the road and glanced at her niece. “He does. Why? Would you like his number?”

Amari turned and looked out the window. “I’m not going to call him. I just want to add more contacts in my phone, that’s all.”

“Are you sure that’s it?”

Amari bit her bottom lip in a failed attempt to keep from smiling. “Where’s the house?” Amari asked, changing the subject.

Iman pulled up to a curb and put her car in park. She looked around with a frown on her face. She remembered exactly where Ms. Bessie lived because it wasn’t far from the grocery store she often frequented. She looked down at her ringing phone and connected to the Bluetooth speakers before answering. “Hello, Mr. Anderson,” she said to one of the men from the home improvement company.

“Mrs. Carrington, the address you gave us doesn’t exist.”

“What do you mean it doesn’t exist?”

“The street does, but that address isn’t in the phone book nor my GPS. I’ve driven up and down the street. I don’t see it.”

Am I losing my mind? Iman thought.

“I apologize for the trouble. Let me see if I can locate her and I will give you a call back.”

“What are you going to do?” Amari asked.

“I have no idea. This is strange. I know this is where I brought her that day.” She looked around the area. “I remember the houses on each side of her. Those are the same cars I saw that day." Iman remembered the day she thought she saw Micah and Candi together. That'd turned out to be a dream. Could she have imagined Ms. Bessie? But why would she imagine talking to an old lady? Not once but twice.

"Do you remember seeing me talking with an older lady the day we volunteered at Damascus?"

Amari shook her head.

"Come on. Remember? I was about to go in the back and help make desserts. You asked to come with me and I told you to help Leah out."

"I remember asking, but I don't recall seeing an older lady."

I must be losing it. Iman put her car in gear and drove off.

They arrived at Damascus and walked inside. She spotted Leah and walked up to her. "Hey, Leah."

Leah offered a polite smile. "Hey."

"I owe you an apology. You were right about everything. I've been a horrible friend. Stop by the house tonight if you get a chance. We're having a few friends over. Nothing fancy. Just hors' d'oeuvres, Christmas music, maybe some movies and games."

"I'd love to come. I've been meaning to call and thank you for the thoughtful gift. I was a little hard on you. It was me, not you. God had me on assignment and I got my emotions involved."

"What do you mean?"

"When you first started at the detention center, God began showing me things about you, not in detail, but I prayed for you often and He often prompted me to talk to you; you know, be a listening ear. I guess after all these years, I thought. I don't know…"

Iman touched her arm. "I get it and I do consider you a friend. I didn't know how to be that. I hate showing emotion. I feel like I always have to be strong. I've been that way my whole life. Don't give up on me."

Leah smiled. "Never." The women hugged.

"You come here often," Iman said. "Do you know an older woman named Bessie?"

Leah turned her head to the side and looked ahead. She shook her head. "No. Doesn't ring a bell."

"She comes and volunteers a few days a week."

"I know everyone that comes in and out, and there's no one by that name."

"Maybe she goes by something else." Iman described her, but Leah had no memory of her.

"Maybe she's an angel."

Iman turned to Amari, who'd just appeared. "This isn't a Hallmark special. Angels don't walk around in human form and they sure don't need canes and live in raggedy houses."

Amari shrugged. *"Be not forgetful to entertain strangers: for thereby, some have entertained angels unaware."*

Iman and Leah both looked at Amari with their mouths open.

"And that's the word." She turned and walked away.

"I like her," Leah said.

Iman's eyes beamed with pride. "She's something special, isn't she?"

Chapter *Twenty-Six*

"The house looks amazing," Amari said while turning in a full circle. "We did good."

"I'll say." Vivian walked in and placed the grocery bags on the kitchen counter. "You went all out, didn't you?"

"Hey, Nana." Amari walked up and hugged Vivian. They'd grown very close over the past few weeks. Vivian was thrilled to have her first grandchild. She never had the chance to play the grandma role with Iman.

Iman looked around. "Is it too much?"

"Not at all. I'm glad you're getting into the holiday spirit."

The tree was beautifully decorated in red and gold with tons of presents underneath. The dining room table was set with red and gold placemats, china, and a poinsettia in the center. White and gold candles were strategically placed throughout the formal dining area and living room. The fireplace was on. Fake snow, lights, and ribbon were around the mantle.

"I have a lot to be grateful for," Iman said, looking at Amari.

The door opened and in walked Maya with a box. "Merry Christmas, ladies." The women embraced.

"What do you have there?" Iman asked.

"A few dishes I whipped up."

"I told you not to bring anything. We're only having a few finger foods."

"Girl, it's Christmas Eve and I'm hungry. Is Micah back yet?"

"He should be here in about an hour. He says he has a surprise. I can't wait to see what it is."

Amari kept glancing in the direction of the living room.

"Who are you looking for?" Iman asked. Amari looked back down at her phone without responding.

Iman pulled her gaze from Amari and turned to Maya. "Where's my nephew?"

"He'll be inside in a few. He's getting the rest of the bags from the car."

Iman glanced at Amari. "Hear that? He'll be inside in a few."

Amari's eyes grew wide. "Huh? Who? I wasn't…" She sat on a barstool and lowered her head.

"Y'all stop embarrassing my baby," Vivian said.

Amari pushed a few buttons on her phone and then stood and headed towards the stairs.

"Where are you going? We'll stop."

"I'm have to get something from my room."

Iman shook her head. "I remember my first crush," she sighed. "To be a kid again."

"Again?" Vivian said. "I don't recall you ever being a kid."

"What was she like as a child?" Maya asked.

"Stubborn. Too independent for her own good." Vivian laughed. "She was smart as a whip though and focused. I never had to worry about her. Never gave us any problems."

Iman smiled and gave Vivian a kiss on the cheek.

Maya looked around. "Where is that boy? He should've been in here." She went to the front door and opened it. Tyler was standing on the passenger side of their car leaned against the door looking down at his phone. "What are you doing?"

"Give me a minute, Ma."

"Why?"

"Ma."

"Hurry up."

"What was that about?" Iman asked.

"Girl, I don't know. On that phone again. He spent over an hour in the bathroom getting ready and begged me to stop by the store so he could get some new cologne."

Iman's brows went up. "Really?"

"Yes. And then made me wait outside. He didn't want his mommy helping him shop." Maya rolled her eyes. "But, you know me. I had to know what he'd gotten. So, I stopped at a gas station and had him pump the gas. I looked in the bag and was shocked. He bought *Invictus*. That cologne is about $80."

"What?" Iman said. "Where'd he get that kind of money?"

"He's been holding on to his allowance, birthday money and so on for years. All of a sudden, he's buying new clothes and spending money on cologne."

"Must be a girl," Vivian said.

"It's definitely a girl. Because I kept looking and saw another box. And unless it was for me, which I'm sure it's not, because I found my Christmas gift from him in his closet yesterday."

Iman swatted her. "Girl, you are a mess." She laughed.

"Anyway. He's gone and bought somebody some Coach Poppy perfume."

"Boy's got some good taste," Iman said. "That's one of my favorites."

Amari walked into the kitchen and did a quick turn towards the family room without looking in their direction.

"Where are you going?" Iman hollered after her. "I thought you wanted to help us out in here. And what's in your hand?" They heard the screen door open and close.

"She's probably going out to talk to Tyler. They've always gotten along well," Maya said.

"I don't know. I think she has a little crush on him."

Vivian stopped moving around the kitchen and looked at them. "You two are sad." She shook her head. "Just sad."

"What?" they asked in unison.

"I knew she liked him from the first time I saw them together. She couldn't keep her eyes off of him the day we took them to Dave & Buster's. Some kids from his school showed up, some of which were girls. Amari's entire mood changed after that. The rest of the day, she had an attitude. Barely said two words to him."

"Wow," Iman said. "It's more serious than I thought." She grunted. "I'm not ready for this."

"What?" Vivian asked.

"The heartbreak. She just lost her mom. When she finds out Tyler is into someone else, she's going to be crushed."

Vivian shook her head. "That girl is just like you. She can handle it."

"I hope so."

"What would it take to get you to move up here permanently? I think I need some extra eyes with a teenager living here."

Vivian laughed. "You don't need an old lady invading your space. She's a good girl. You'll be fine. Now, if you had three or four running around, that'd be a different story."

"Hey, ladies." Leah walked in and sat her bags down on the table. "The door was open. Hope you don't mind me coming on in."

"I'm glad you could come." Iman stood from her seat and hugged her. "What's all this?"

"I bought a few things for the kids. But, wait until tomorrow to open it."

"You didn't have to go through the trouble."

"Glad to do it."

"You remember Maya."

"Yeah." The women embraced. "We see each other often at Damascus."

"Oh yeah. I forgot. The two good Samaritans."

Iman turned to Vivian. "This is my mom, Vivian Braswell. Mom, this is my good friend, Leah. We work together."

She didn't miss the bright smile displayed across Leah's face after addressing her as a good friend.

"I'm glad my baby has such good friends."

"Who's the boy your niece is out there talking to?"

Iman and Maya looked at each other. "What were they doing?" Maya asked.

"Leaned against the car. When I drove up, it looked like they were exchanging gifts."

The screen door opened and in walked Tyler and Amari into the kitchen as if nothing out of the ordinary had taken place. Tyler sat the boxes of food on the table and Amari sat on the barstool next to Iman.

Maya took out her pie plates from the box and placed them around the table designated for desserts. "You get everything?"

"Yes ma'am," Amari said. "The gifts are next to the tree and—" She leaned away from Iman and frowned. "What are you doing?"

"You smell good. You been in my perfume?"

Maya watched the exchange in silence. Amari bit her bottom lip to keep from smiling. "No."

Maya and Iman made eye contact and smiled.

"Something smells good." Tyler walked into the kitchen, sampling the different dishes.

"That's what we were saying," Maya said.

Oblivious to the ladies conversation, Tyler pulled the top off the fried chicken. "I'm hungry. When are we going to eat?"

"Get on out of this kitchen messing with this food." Maya walked towards him. "You haven't even washed your hands."

Tyler grabbed a wing and stuck it in his mouth before his mom reached him.

"You'll eat soon enough. We're waiting for Uncle Micah to get home."

"It's fine," Iman said. "He can have a little something to tide him over."

"Thanks, Auntie." He kissed Iman on the cheek before grabbing another piece of chicken.

Chapter *Twenty-Seven*

"We wish you a Merry Christmas. We wish you a merry Christmas—"

Iman rushed and opened the front door. "Look guys!" She yelled. "Carolers."

All the women rushed to the door and listened, as a group of students from the neighborhood school walked and sang Christmas songs.

"This makes me think of us singing in the kitchen every Christmas Eve."

Vivian smiled. "That was always your favorite."

"You sing?" Leah asked.

"You look surprised." Iman laughed. "I used to sing."

"She got a voice like an angel," Vivian said.

"I really don't know you, do I?" Leah chuckled.

"Don't feel bad," Maya chimed in. "I've never heard her sing either."

Vivian frowned. "Chile. You let everything go, didn't you?"

"Why is it that every time we have gatherings, the attention turns to me?"

"You're just so darn interesting," Maya said.

"Whatever." She smacked her lips. "Speaking of interesting, why didn't you bring Lawrence?"

Maya's smile grew wide and she turned her head away from everyone.

"Who's Lawrence?" Leah asked.

"Maya's new man."

"He is not my man. We met at church and we've gone out on a few dates and most were group dates. That's it."

"I may need to visit you guys' church. Because the men at my church are blah." Leah turned her thumb upside down.

"We got some nice ones at Agape," Iman said. "And the singles ministry is amazing. I almost hated to get married because I wanted to keep attending."

"Speaking of married, "Maya said, "wasn't Micah supposed to be here by now?"

Iman glanced at the clock on the wall. "You're right." She picked up her phone. "I'll call his cell."

Iman dialed his number and stepped out of the room. "His phone went to voicemail." She sat on the arm of the sofa and leaned her head against the wall.

Maya and Vivian stopped and observed Iman. Each looked as if they were searching for the right thing to say.

"I'm sure he's fine, baby. Don't you go worrying." Vivian sat down beside her. "It's Christmas Eve. I'm sure the airports are crowded. His plane probably got delayed."

"Pull his itinerary," Leah said. "I'll call the airline and check for flight delays."

"Good idea," Maya said.

Iman pulled up the email and forwarded it to Leah's phone. "I'll step into the kitchen and call."

Maya and Vivian looked as if they were afraid she'd start to panic.

"I'm okay. I have to believe God has him." They didn't move. "Seriously, guys. I'm okay."

Chapter *Twenty-Eight*

"Silent Night. Holy Night."

The women looked at each other, trying to figure out where the beautiful melody came from.

"Is that a CD?" Maya asked.

"It's coming from the kitchen," Vivian said.

The three ladies stood in the kitchen with their mouths opened. Nobody said anything. Amari stood with her back turned to everyone and earphones in her ears.

She stopped singing and removed her earphones. She picked up her plate and turned to see she had an audience. Her eyebrows dipped and her mouth and nose turned up. "Why are you all staring at me like that?" She walked passed them and went into the family room, sat on the sofa and ate her food.

They turned to follow her. "I didn't know you could sing like that," Iman said.

Amari shrugged. "What's the big deal?"

Vivian laughed. "Ooooh Lord, this girl is too much like you."

Iman sat next to Amari and took her plate and sat it on the table. “Hey,” Amari protested.

“Hush up and come here. You too, Mama.”

They walked over to the grand piano that hadn’t been used in years. “I don’t know how this is going to sound.”

Vivian sat down and hit a few notes. “Leah. Maya. Tyler. Come on over here.”

“I don’t sing,” Tyler said.

“Me either,” Maya and Leah said in unison.

“Don’t matter. Stand around us and move your lips.”

Vivian played a C chord. “Could use a tune up, but I can work with it. “Here are your notes. *C E G.*” She called each person’s name before hitting each note. “C -That’s my note. E-Iman. G-Amari. *Silent Night*. You ready?” They nodded.

“What’s my note?” Maya asked.

Vivian turned and looked at her, as if to say don’t interrupt me. “Sing whatever you feel.”

Maya and Leah looked at each other and laughed.

Vivian played a few notes and everyone sang in perfect harmony. After they finished a few rounds of *Silent Night*, they sang *Away In a Manger and Joy to the World*. Now they were singing Iman’s favorite, *I’ll Be Home for Christmas.* They’d gotten so into it, when the doorbell rang, they didn’t realize forty-five minutes had passed and Leah was gone.

"I wonder who that could be," Iman said. Vivian continued to play softly while Amari hummed.

"Micah, maybe?" Maya offered.

Iman frowned. "Why would he knock?"

The two women went to the door and looked outside.

"That's strange," Maya said. "Nobody's out there."

They closed the door and moved towards the kitchen. The back door opened and Micah walked inside.

Iman ran into his arms. "Oh my goodness. I'm happy to see you. I was worried something had happened."

Micah's eyes danced as he stared at his wife. "I'm fine, baby."

Iman let go and stood back and watched Micah's expression. It was difficult to read. He stood there, staring.

"Micah, you're scaring me. What's wrong? It's Solei, isn't it? Is she suing you? Trying to get alimony?" Iman started pacing. "She wants you back, doesn't she?"

"Whoa. Calm down, baby." He rubbed his hands down her arms. "Remember I said I had a surprise for you?"

"Yeah," she said slowly. She looked around him. "Where is it?"

"Outside."

"Can the suspense already, Micah. Get on with it," Maya said from the other side of the kitchen.

Micah stepped aside and Leah walked in with two little boys who looked like smaller versions of Micah.

Iman stared at the little boys who'd wrapped their arms around Micah's legs and were holding on for life. So many thoughts ran through her mind. There was no question of family resemblance, but who were they? Nephews? Cousins? They looked to be about three and a half or four, so the possibility of him stepping outside of their marriage wasn't the case.

"Are you going to say anything?" Micah asked.

"What? Where? Who?" She scratched her head. "Are they staying?"

"My dream!" Amari shouted when she walked into the kitchen. "Those are the boys from my dream. I always wanted brothers." She walked up and reached her hands out. "Hey guys. You want some pie?" They both nodded and put their hands in hers.

"You made that look too easy," Micah said.

Iman's eyes followed the little boys, until Micah's voice captured her attention.

"Meet our sons."

Chapter *Twenty-Nine*

After everyone fixed their plates, they each sat around the table. Everyone was eating except for Iman, whose eyes remained glued to the twins until they disappeared with their food into the family room with Tyler and Amari.

Once they were out of sight, Iman watched her husband stuff his mouth, as if this was a normal day. He finally looked up. "What?"

"How can you sit there eating?" She looked around. "How can all of you sit there stuffing your faces, as if my husband didn't just come inside with two little boys who looks exactly like him and call them our sons?"

"Because we're hungry," Maya said. "Besides, I figure that heffa was probably pregnant when she left. But, as usual, her sorry selfish behind didn't say anything until she had no choice."

Everyone looked to Micah for reassurance. "Is that what happened?" Iman asked.

He shrugged. "Pretty much." He continued to eat.

Iman stood brusquely and pulled his plate from in front of him. “I can’t stand this, Micah. You have to tell me more information.”

“Babe. I’m hungry. I haven’t eaten since breakfast. Let me finish eating and then I’ll tell you everything.” He reached for his plate, and she put it behind her back and stepped away.

“Talk, then eat.”

Micah picked up a napkin and wiped his mouth. “She and her boyfriend had been going from city to city robbing banks. They’d been doing it for almost a year. Her boyfriend got arrested and she knew it wouldn’t be long before she would be next. To keep from having the boys placed in the system, she decided it was time I knew I had children and she wanted me to come get them.”

Iman slumped in her chair. “It’s just bank robbery. She didn’t kill anyone. She’ll probably do a few years and then she’ll be back to claim her children, right?”

Micah shook his head. “No, baby. I wouldn’t let that happen to you again. I made her relinquish all her rights. David’s sources told him they were about to be taken from her anyway. She rarely had them. They were usually with someone else. Besides,” he grabbed a roll from the middle of the table and bit off a piece, “she’ll be in longer than a few years. Someone ended up having a heart attack during the last break-in and someone was shot at another. She’s being charged with aggravated assault, armed robbery, endangerment, and a host of other things. They're ours."

Iman sat back in her chair. It finally started to sink in. She'd gone from having no children to three in weeks. Tears rolled down her face and Micah reached up and wiped them away.

"Are those tears of joy?" He asked.

She nodded and smiled.

He reached in front of her and pulled his plate towards him. "Good. Now, can I eat?"

"What's their names?" Maya asked.

Micah smiled. "Micah Andrew and Jonathan Isaiah."

"Looks like she stuck with the names you always wanted," Iman said.

Micah shrugged.

"The boys are tired," Amari said, walking into the kitchen. "You want me to get them ready for bed?"

Iman stood. "Sure, sweetie." She turned to Micah. "Do they have pajamas?"

He nodded his head in the direction of the luggage he'd brought in. "In that bag over there."

Tyler walked into the room and stood next to Amari. They looked at each other a long while. Micah stopped eating and watched the exchange.

"You need some help?" Tyler asked.

Micah stood abruptly almost knocking his chair over. "No. She doesn't need help. You get on back in there and play Mario Bros. or something and, when I come back down, we're going to talk."

Vivian stood and stopped Micah. "You've been away from your family all day. I'll take care of the boys." Vivian and Amari grabbed one child each and headed upstairs.

Iman watched as Vivian took her three children upstairs and didn't take her eyes away until they disappeared around the corner. She turned her head to find three smiling faces watching her in amusement.

She scrunched her nose. "Why are you guys staring at me like that?"

"This is exciting." Maya stood and embraced Iman with tears in her eyes. "Not only do you get to experience being a mom, you can finally have the Christmas experience you deserve."

"It still hasn't completely sunk in. It seems unreal. Like I'm going to wake up from a dream at any minute." Iman wiped the tears that had trickled down her face. This is definitely the best Christmas I've ever..."

Iman gasped and covered her mouth.

"What's wrong?" Micah asked.

"It's Christmas Eve and we don't have any gifts for the boys to open tomorrow. I'm sure everything's closed already."

"Is that all?" He grabbed another piece of chicken.

"Is that all?" Iman repeated. "That's major. I don't want their first Christmas with us to be—"

"It's taken care of."

Iman watched Micah's gaze turn to Leah, and they both smiled. Iman and Maya looked back and forth between the two.

"What don't I know?"

"I called Leah yesterday and told her about the boys. I asked her to pick up a few things."

Iman stared at her husband in disbelief. When she'd spoken with Leah at Damascus this morning, she'd already had plans to come to their Christmas Eve dinner.

She looked at Leah. "So, this morning when I saw you—"

"Yep." Leah nodded. "I was planning to call and apologize. I could only hope you would take the bait and invite me."

"Didn't you notice Leah walked in with the boys?" Micah asked.

"I'm offended." Maya directed her attention to Micah. "You didn't let me in on it."

"Because you would've hung up and called Iman as soon as we got off the phone."

Maya shook her head. "I'm hurt. I'm deeply hurt."

"There's nothing about you that's deep."

Maya picked up a roll and threw it across the table at Micah.

Chapter *Thirty*

Iman sat up in her bed and turned her head towards Micah. She slapped his arm, but he didn't move. She pushed his shoulder back and forth until he stirred. "Micah." His head shot up. "What's wrong? You okay?"

"Good, you're up. I had the strangest dream."

He looked at the clock. "It's five in the morning. You woke me up because of a dream? Is it the same one you'd been having?"

"No, listen. It felt so real. I dreamed you came home with two little boys and said they were your sons Solei never told you about. You said she was pregnant when she left and the only reason she told you was because she was in jail and didn't want them in foster care."

"That's interesting," Micah said. "Why don't you go and check on Amari."

Iman frowned. "Why?"

"It's Christmas. I'm sure she's ready to open her gifts."

Iman stretched and sat up on the side of the bed. "You coming?"

"Yeah. After I use the bathroom."

Iman walked down the hall and opened Amari's bedroom door. She squeezed her eyes shut and opened them again. Amari was asleep on the floor wrapped in a pink sleeping bag, and the two little boys from her dream were in bed.

A smile crept up on Iman's face. *It wasn't a dream.*

Seconds later, she felt her husband's strong, yet gentle caress down her arms. He encircled her waist from behind.

"This is the best day of my life. The only thing that would make this day better is if I were to walk downstairs and see Mama in the kitchen cooking her traditional Christmas morning breakfast. Bacon. Sausage. Ham. Scrambled eggs. Grits. Homemade biscuits."

Amari opened her eyes and squinted. "Do you always make a habit of watching me sleep? Because it's creepy." She rolled over and pulled the sleeping bag over her face.

"I don't know," Micah said. "We thought you may want to open your gifts before we head out for church this morning. We're going to early morning service."

Before Micah could get the word 'gifts' out of his mouth good, Amari was unzipping her sleeping bag, trying to get out.

"Why didn't you say that instead of just standing there?" She stood and went into the bathroom.

Micah and Iman laughed. "Let's get the boys up," he said.

Iman touched Micah's arm. "You know Amari and I both have been having dreams about these children. So far, they've come to pass." She looked down at her feet and then back up at her husband. "But, what about the baby girl? Do you think Destiny will change her mind and give us the baby?"

Micah shrugged. "I can't answer that question, but I do know the word says, "If we delight ourselves in Him, He will give us the desires of our heart." Let's wait on Him and see what He does." He kissed her cheek. "But this time, let's stay out of His way and let Him do it. Agreed?"

She smiled and looked up into his eyes. "Agreed."

"Something smells good," Micah said when he entered the kitchen.

Vivian turned and smiled. "Well, good morning, sleepy heads."

"This is some spread. A brother could get used to this. What would it take for me to convince you to move in permanently?"

"It's a done deal." Iman walked into the kitchen holding the boys' hands. "She told me last night if I had three or four kids, she'd move in." Iman gasped. "You cooked our traditional breakfast?"

“Of course I did. Just because you stopped celebrating didn’t mean I stopped.

“You moving in, Nana Vi?” Amari walked into the kitchen with her braids pulled up into a high bun, dressed in skinny jeans and a red sweater.

“No, baby. That’s just wishful thinking on your Auntie’s part.” She looked up at Amari over her glasses. “Don’t you look nice?”

“Thanks.”

“You’re not wearing that to church, are you?” Micah asked.

“No. This is my pre-church attire. You guys are going to take pictures of me while I open my gifts, so I can post them to Instagram and Snapchat.”

“Before we do any of that, let’s give thanks. And don’t forget to use the grateful jar. Come on. Let’s join hands and pray.” Iman looked around. “Where are the boys?”

Moving from room to room, everyone started looking around. “Found them!” Amari yelled. “We’re in the family room.”

Everyone rushed in at once.

“Looks like someone didn’t want to wait for prayer and breakfast,” Micah said.

Gift-wrap paper was strewn across the floor. They’d successfully opened most of their gifts as well as a few others.

“Drum,” Micah Jr. said.

“Truck,” Jonathan said.

“We want to play,” they said in unison.

"Pray first. Then play," Micah said while lifting them up, placing each one under an arm like two footballs.

"No! No!" they yelled and kicked. "We want to play!"

Amari, who seemed oblivious to what was happening, held her phone up in front of her. She was spinning and backing and walking to the side, trying to find the perfect lighting to snap a selfie.

Vivian had turned and gone back into the kitchen.

Iman stood in the doorway in plain view of the kitchen and family room with a satisfied smile on her face. She finally had everything she'd ever wanted. Though she still hoped for a baby girl one day, she was grateful.

Nothing could top this Christmas. No matter what happened, she couldn't be brought down. This Christmas overshadowed all of the pain and suffering she'd experienced every Christmas prior. Nothing could take away the joy she felt at that moment.

The boys still yelling and kicking in his arms, Micah looked at Iman. "What are you just standing there for?"

"Look at them. We have a real life teen and two preschoolers."

"Well, can you come in here and help me with these real life preschoolers so we can pray, eat, and open some gifts?"

"Don't you think that's a bit much for her?" Micah asked Iman as he watched Amari open one of her many gifts.

Iman had thought the same thing while she wrapped the gifts a few days prior. Not only had she given her the latest iPhone, she had an iPad, iPod touch, top notch art supplies, three pairs of shoes, ten new outfits, and seven books by her favorite author. She almost bought her a television for her room but didn't, for fear she would never come out.

Growing up, Iman usually got three gifts at Christmas. She wasn't sure if it was because Jesus was given three gifts the day He was born or if that was just what her grandparents chose, but she could do more and she felt Amari deserved more this year. Although she didn't act like she was too heartbroken and was seemingly dealing with the loss extremely well, losing a parent was never easy. She kept her eyes glued to the boys playing with their toys and the huge smile on Amari's face while she opened her gifts. "She deserves it."

"Promise me that this is it. You don't have to buy her love. She already loves you and she's forgiven you." He kissed her on the cheek and sat on the floor in the midst of the children.

Their home phone rang.

"Can you get the phone, Ma?" Iman called out to Vivian, who was in the kitchen clearing away the breakfast dishes. For once, she wasn't worried about who was calling them on their landline early on Christmas morning. It didn't matter. Life was finally perfect.

"Can one of you take me to the hospital?" Vivian asked out of breath. "It's Tina. It's doesn't sound good."

Chapter *Thirty-One*

"We're here to see Tiana Sawyer," Iman said as soon as she and Vivian reached the patient registration counter.

Micah was on his way to take Amari and the boys to Maya's and then he would meet them at the hospital.

The receptionist placed her finger on the computer keyboard and typed in the name. "Are you relatives?"

"Yes," Vivian spoke up. "I'm her auntie and this is her cousin."

"Names," the receptionist said with little interest.

"I'm Iman Carrington."

"Carrington?" The receptionist said. "She's been asking for you. I was told to send you right in when you arrived. She has you down as next of kin."

Iman's face scrunched into a frown. Tiana had two living parents and a host of siblings. The list of aunts, uncles, and cousins could go on for eternity. Iman wondered why her of all people? They'd spoken. Sure, she didn't give

Tiana a chance to ask the favor she'd intended to ask, but she'd forgiven her. Surely that wasn't why she needed her there. Iman's heart had softened towards her. Their relationship would never be as it once was, but she cared about her well-being. She'd told her she had HIV. That used to be a death sentence, but because of the advances in technology with the right medical care, it wasn't unheard of for people to live full and productive lives.

The receptionist paged the nurse and let her know Vivian and Iman were there to see Tiana.

"One of our nurses will be out shortly to escort you to Ms. Sawyer's room."

Vivian and Iman stole glances at each other before addressing the receptionist. "She's in a room?' Vivian asked. "Wasn't she just rushed to the emergency room?"

"Yes. She came in a few hours ago, but she's already been assigned a room."

"So, she's okay?" Iman asked.

"Hi," the nurse said as soon as she approached the ladies. "I'm Cheryl. I want to speak with you before we go inside. Tiana left specific instructions to have you," she looked directly at Iman, "come in alone."

"Is she okay? Is she alert? What's going on?"

"Oh yes," the nurse reassured her. "She's alert."

Iman's eyes pleaded with Vivian to come in with her.

"Go on," Vivian said. "I'll be right out here if you need me."

The nurse walked away, and Vivian stepped to the side and got a drink of water. Iman put her hand on the doorknob, inhaled, and said a quick prayer. She didn't know what to expect on the other side of the door. For once, she wasn't going to overthink this; she wasn't going to think of an escape plan. She would go inside, find out what was going on, and trust that God would guide her to handle anything that was thrown her way.

Iman walked in slowly and gave Tiana a once over. There was an IV in her arm and a machine next to her bed monitoring her blood pressure and heart rate. Tiana's back was to her and she wasn't moving.

Iman walked closer to the bed and gently placed her arm on Tiana's shoulder. "Tiana head and squinted until Iman's face came into view. She offered a small smile. "You came?" she whispered.

Iman reached behind her and grabbed a chair and pulled it close to Tiana's bed. She sat and waited, as Tiana struggled to roll over and face her. "You put me as next of kin?" Iman's eyebrow raised and she smiled.

Tiana nodded. "In case I die." She started coughing uncontrollably. Iman stood and grabbed a cup from a nearby table and poured water in it from the pitcher on the cabinet.

She waited for Tiana to finish drinking and placed it on the counter. She sat back down beside her and put her hand in Tiana's.

"What do you need from me?" Iman asked.

Tiana squeezed her eyes shut and breathed in and out repeatedly for a few seconds. "My baby girl. She needs a stable home." Tears rolled down Tiana's face. "She needs you."

Iman wasn't sure how to respond. She had no idea Tiana had a child. Vivian couldn't have known or she would've told her. "Does anyone else know about this?"

Tiana shook her head. "No one in our family knows. Aunt Vi knows about the HIV, but no-one knows I have a baby." She reached for the remote that controlled her bed.

Iman handed it to her and waited while she sat her head up and got comfortable.

"After the fiasco with Cedric, everyone started treating me differently. He and I messed around for a few months, but after that, he moved on with someone else. That's when I moved to Phoenix."

"You were in Phoenix?" This was news to Iman. For all she knew, Tiana still lived in Georgia as if nothing had changed. She'd spent all those years away from her family thinking she would run into Tiana.

Tiana nodded. "I was too ashamed to stay around." She cleared her throat and pointed to the water pitcher. Iman stood and poured her another cup full and handed it to her.

"After a few months, I met a really nice guy, at least I thought so at first. We dated, got engaged and I got pregnant. When I went for my first appointment, they tested me for everything, as is routine for pregnant women. That's when I found out I had HIV."

Iman's eyes grew wide.

"Don't worry," Tiana said. "Sarah doesn't have it."

"You named her Sarah?"

Tiana nodded. "You used to love that name. I wasn't sure if you still did. You can change it if you like."

Iman was surprised that Tiana remembered such a minor detail. She'd long forgotten.

"So, you—"

"Yeah." She nodded. "I never wanted children, you know that. Besides, I'm far too sick to take care of a child. I'm in and out of this hospital so much, I wouldn't be any good to her."

"Where is she now?"

"She's been with a foster family since the day she was born."

This was a lot for Iman to process. She'd been given not one but three children within a month's time. She wasn't sure she could take on an infant so soon. "Where's the father?"

Tiana turned her head and faced the window. "Dead."

"Oh, Ti. I'm sorry to hear that."

"Don't be. He knew he was infected before he met me. He died in prison."

The women sat in silence.

"I don't want her to know about us," Tiana finally said. "As far as anyone is concerned, you and Micah are her parents."

"This is a lot to process, Ti. I need to pray about this and I need to talk to Micah." Iman stood and went to the door. She turned back to Tiana and said, "What do I tell Mama? She's right outside the door. She's waiting to see you."

"Send her in. I'll talk to her."

Chapter *Thirty-Two*

"I'm still not sure about this," Iman said as she sat at the kitchen table looking over the legal documents she and Micah had just gone over. As soon as Iman left Tiana's room, she called Micah and filled him in. Instead of coming to the hospital, he called David and had him look into it. As always, David came through. Never mind that it was Christmas Sunday, he would deliver at any given moment. He'd gotten in touch with Tiana's lawyer, as well as the foster parents and the social worker. Everything Tiana said had checked out.

Micah grabbed the stack of papers and placed them back inside the folder. He put his fist under his chin and leaned onto the table, giving his wife his undivided attention. "Isn't this the missing piece to the puzzle? You've asked God for four children. He's been showing you and Amari a baby girl. What's the problem?"

Iman stood and walked to the window and looked out into the backyard. She turned and looked back at Micah. "What if it's too much? What if I can't do it? You see how I get when I'm stressed." She looked towards the stairs and lowered her voice. "The drinking. The pills. Amari is interested in boys. I haven't even had the chance to bond with the twins yet. What if they don't take to me right away? What if—"

"We can go over what ifs all day." Micah stood and walked to Iman, taking her hand in his. He pulled her into his arms and held her tight. "Mama Vi is here. I'm here. And I've seen you in action with teens far worse than Amari would ever think to be. You can do this. We can do this. Are you sure there's not something else holding you back? Have you forgiven Tiana?"

Iman was silent. She laid her head on Micah's chest for a long while before saying anything. "It's not that."

"Then, what is it?"

"It's Amari."

Micah backed away and looked down at his wife. "Amari?"

"She told me that when Kendall, Karlos, and Kaitlyn were here, she felt I stopped loving her. Infants need lots of attention. What if she starts to feel that way again? I don't want to hurt her anymore."

"You should do it."

Micah and Iman looked up to see Amari on the bottom step.

"What are you doing up? And how long have you been standing there eavesdropping?" Micah released Iman and turned to Amari.

"I couldn't sleep."

"You okay?" Iman moved closer to Amari and felt her head. "Are you sick?"

She shook her head.

"Are the twins keeping you up? We're going to get them their own beds in the morning so you can—"

"They don't bother me. I like having them in there. Remember when you said I can talk to you about anything?"

Iman nodded slowly. "Yes."

"Should I leave?" Iman and Amari both turned when Micah spoke, as if they'd forgotten he was there.

Amari shrugged. "You can if you want. It's about sex though."

Micah's eyebrows dipped and his face tensed. "I hope it's hypothetical."

"You're too easy," Amari said. She looked up at Iman. "I never apologized for my attitude towards you when I first came here."

"You don't have to—"

"Yes, I do," Amari interrupted. "I was wrong and Mom taught me to apologize when I'm wrong. I was disrespectful."

Iman squeezed onto the step beside Amari and put her arm around her but didn't say anything.

"I'm not having sex and I'm not thinking about it. That's something I'm waiting to do when I'm married."

"Yes." Micah threw his hand in the air as if he was giving God a fist bump. Iman looked at him and playfully rolled her eyes.

"I made that promise to Mom before she died. She was tired of living and the only thing she cared about was that I was taken care of, and she knew without a doubt that you and Uncle Micah would take me in and treat me as if I were yours."

Iman batted her eyes quickly to keep the tears from falling.

"My well-being was all she cared about. Whenever she thought I wasn't listening, I heard her on the phone with her lawyer, and sometimes when she prayed." Amari stopped and swallowed the lump that had started to build in her throat. She wiped her tears. By this time, everyone was crying. She allowed her body to rest against Iman's. "You may have other reasons for not wanting this baby, but don't do it because you think I can't handle it because I can and I won't be a handful. If Ms. Tiana is anything like mom was, she just wants her baby taken care of. I'll help out around the house. I'll help out with the kids and—"

Iman rubbed her hand up and down Amari's arm. "That's not your job. Your only job is to be a kid. If we do decide to get Sarah, you will be the big sister, not the babysitter, not the mom. Understand?"

She nodded.

"I know that's right."

Everyone looked to the top of the stairs where Vivian stood. "I can't stand how these mamas make their oldest responsible for the younger ones like they're the ones that had them. Lazy behinds." Vivian walked down the stairs and sat a few stairs up from Iman and Amari.

"But, that's a different story for me. I'll stay and help until you tell me to go."

"Really?" Iman squeaked. "You're staying?"

"Truth be told, I felt kind of cheated out of being a grandma. Not only has God blessed you with three, maybe four beautiful children, He's given me my desire of being a Nana."

Epilogue

(Five Weeks Later)

Agape Christian Fellowship was usually packed on Sunday's, but it was an especially tight fit on this particular Sunday. Iman couldn't remember the last time she'd seen the ushers bringing in chairs from the fellowship hall. Not only were the regular attendees and guests there, many of her former co-workers were also present, as well as many of her family members that she hadn't seen in seven years.

The adoption had been finalized three days ago. Micah and Iman didn't want to waste anytime having Sarah and the boys dedicated. Amari was dedicated as a baby, but she wanted to be very hands on with her younger siblings. She chose their outfits. Iman had invited Tiana to come and share in the joyous occasion but, as she looked around the sanctuary, she didn't see her. Though Tiana gave up her rights and didn't want anyone to know she was the biological mother of Sarah, Iman was open to her being a part of their lives, even if it were only as a cousin, but she wanted no part in it. Tiana had plans to leave town but wouldn't say where she was would be living. The only reason she'd stuck around Maryland as long as she had was to be sure her daughter ended up with the family she'd chosen for her. She thought that was the least she could do as a mother.

Cheers, whistles, and applause were heard throughout the building after Dr. C. and her husband, Pastor Joel, anointed and prayed for the family. Some of the members dismissed themselves into the fellowship hall to set up the dinner the church had prepared for the Carrington's and their family and friends. Those who were still inside had formed a line to walk around and greet the family. There wasn't a dry eye on the altar and very few in the congregation. Maya stood alongside Micah, Iman, Vivian, and Amari as Godmother, and David, Micah's good friend and attorney, stood as the Godfather.

There was no other word to describe how Iman felt at that moment except for pure joy. Not happiness because that was temporary. The joy she felt was the type of joy that only came from God. Not only had He given her four beautiful children, He'd also given her new lenses. She understood the song that said I once was blind but now I see. Looking out at the number of people there to support her, who were genuinely happy for her, she realized how much she has and had always had.

She did one final sweep of the audience and stopped upon seeing a mean scowl on Lawrence's face. She followed his gaze and landed on David, who was watching Maya with keen interest. She leaned over and whispered to Maya. "How serious are you about Lawrence?"

"I don't know. I like him a lot, why?"

"Because it looks like he's staking claim on you and he doesn't look happy about your new admirer."

Maya's eyes darted back and forth around the room. "What admirer?"

Iman leaned her head to the side towards David. "The Godfather and I think he's got it bad."

Maya smiled. "Ooooh, this is going to be fun."

About the Author

Unlike many authors and others in various professions, Cassie Edwards Whitlow didn't discover at five years old, that she wanted to be an author. She spent a great deal of her childhood and young adult life writing songs and pursuing a music career. It wasn't until her twenties that she discovered her love for writing stories. During her early writing career, she has released to inspirational novels, "Temptation" and "One Wish".

Not only does her knowledge and passion of women's mental and physical health issues shine through in her stories, but her relatable characters and expressive storytelling will definitely keep readers turning the pages to find out the outcome for each character.

Cassie received a Bachelor of Science in Criminal Justice from Southern Arkansas University and a Master's in Psychology from Grand Canyon University.

She's also the wife of an Air Force Sergeant and has two children. She's a native of

Camden, Arkansas, but currently resides in the United Kingdom of Great Britain.

If you are interested in getting to know Cassie, she can be follow her on Social media.
https://www.facebook.com/CassieEdwardsWhitlow/
https://www.instagram.com/cassieedwardswhitlow/
https://twitter.com/cewhitlow

Checkout Other Books by Cassie

Temptation
June 2016